refuge

I will say of the Lord,

He is my **refuge** *and my*

fortress: my God; in Him will I trust

Psalms 91:2

Harry "Buddy" Beckett

Artistic Spaces Publishing
Flemingsburg, KY

Credits:
Song: "Falling in Love" © 1999 Harry Beckett
Song: "Today" © 2000 Harry Beckett
Poem: "My Goal" © 1990 Harry Beckett

Notice: This is a work of fiction. Names, characters, places, and incidents are either products of the author's imagination or, if real, are used ficticiously.

Library of Congress Control Number: 2009907316
Subject Headings
      1. Religious Fiction
      2. Romance

     ISBN 10: 0-9796328-4-6
     ISBN 13: 978-0-9796328-4-6

Published by: Artistic Spaces Publishing Company
                 P.O. Box 54
                 Flemingsburg, KY 41041

Printed in the United States of America

A heap of thanks to three earth angels:
Lois Collins Rimmer
Jennifer Lynn Beckett
Mildred Morrison Caldwell

Using their wordsmithing skill, they patiently hammered my rough manuscript on a grammatical anvil to wrought an easy to read story.

This story is dedicated to all who recognize the need to trust in the Lord Jesus Christ. He lovingly pardons earthy consequences; and someday, will gather His own to eternal peace.

Contents

PROLOGUE

Life can include feelings from joy to sadness and sometimes utter despair. Robert Arlington experienced ineffable earthly joy and happiness when he met Mary O'Day. In that glorious tick of time when his eyes first saw Mary, he knew if she would walk with him, his sojourn on planet earth would be a happy trek. During some sweet summer days in Vermont, Robert and Mary's hearts floated on an idyllic breeze crowded with dreams. Those few days were beautiful and filled with the hope they would spend endless tomorrows always together. At times, they soared to unmapped regions of quintessential love. But one sad day, deceiving winds blew them apart.

Seasons moved along in loneliness for Robert and shame for Mary until an angel helped her through an embarrassing and difficult time in her life. Later, Divine Hands gathered scattered dreams and reunited their hearts. But the road of life is sometimes more than rocky. The deceiving winds that once blew Robert and Mary apart were just a mere gale compared to what later happened to them. An inconceivable event, of hurricane force, stripped Robert of his dignity and ripped all the tenderness from his caring heart. In a court of law, he was sentenced to life in prison.

A young lawyer, Ralph Fenny, and his new employee, Michelle Barker, helped Robert with an appeal. Some people believe "not guilty" are the most important two words in the English Language. When Robert met Ralph, he had no expectation of ever hearing those beautiful words from a higher court jury. For a short time after being incarcerated, and while his mind was still numb from the verdict, he did briefly think about freedom. He yearned for a time when he could again be as free as the summer breeze that had brought Mary to him.

Ralph persuaded Robert to tell him how he met Mary and all that happened while they were together. From this revelation, Ralph was hoping to glean some previously overlooked information that could be used as new evidence in petitioning a higher court for Robert's freedom.

As pages are turned, readers can cruise with empathy with Robert and Mary. You can climb to a breathlessly beautiful mountain top experience when they were falling in love. And then later, traverse a valley shoe-top deep with despair.

While Ralph and Michelle Barker gather information for an appeal, you can almost hear the whisper of angel wings as she relates how angels ministered to her through some difficult times in her young Christian life. She made some mistakes in high school, but later asked Jesus to forgive her and to help her do what was right. While working with Ralph on Robert's deposition, she told him how an angel helped provide food and shelter for her and her baby. In the beginning, he was skeptical. His focus in life had been preparing for his career and he had not read the Bible. She was so honest and thankful for Jesus' love that he knew something special had happened to her. Ralph fell in love with Michelle, and through her testimony, also fell in love with Jesus.

Robert's best friend, Mason Dixon, may have taken the form of a Guardian Angel for a brief period and rescued Ellen Cyrus. She was stranded in sin with no apparent hope of escape. Mason gently showed her an honorable way of life she had long forgotten. Jesus forgave *all* her sins and she was gloriously saved from Hell. After Ellen chose her new direction with Jesus, she and Mason were married. A little later when she had to appear before a group of church deacons, she realized that a Christian's new life is not always smooth.

Dear Reader, you may not remember every word she spoke to the deacons, but as she bravely proclaimed the saving power of Jesus, the depth of her thankfulness will long linger in your heart.

The characters portrayed in this story are living between a first breath and an inevitable last breath. Along the way, they encounter temptations and problems that are real. The evidence of angels in their lives bolsters their faith in Jesus' love and makes sweeter His refuge from life's storms that extend to an eternal safe harbor.

The author's prayer is that readers will realize that the continuation of life's earthly road into a peaceful eternity begins with trusting and accepting Jesus' love and His unmerited forgiveness of sins.

CHAPTER ONE

. . . changing directions.

Rosy shafts of light from the afternoon sun decorated a corner of Ralph Fenny's sparsely furnished office. He sat motionless at his desk staring at the dusty light slowly creeping across the old hardwood floor. He looked at the wall clock and a thought escaped from his crowded mind.

"So I'm burning time."

He had sat at his desk almost this entire Friday without much to do except think. Ralph opened his law practice fourteen months earlier and put out his shingle with great pride and enthusiasm. Now, he was at an intersection on his road of life, and he was going to make a turn.

The decision to close his office was easier now than when he first contemplated such a bold move. Ralph had an analytical mind and had carefully and cautiously weighed and considered all the facts and possible consequences of closing.

Money was not his reason to close. From day one net income had been close to nil, so the loss of income from his law practice would not be a deterrent.

When Ralph was seventeen, his father died and left him twenty-three rental units to manage. Money had never been a problem even during college and law school. There was one problem, however, facing Ralph that kept him glued to his chair. His thoughts were becoming dim like the beam of translucent light in the waning sun. How would he tell his mother?

Ralph Fenny walked out of his office at 7:00 p.m. with no joyous expectations in his remaining life. But he did reason that he was no failure—he was just changing directions. Even so, he was uneasy as he started for home. Mother would be upset because "her Ralphy" would be two hours late.

After dinner, his mother, Fern, mentioned that earlier in the day when cleaning she had found an old newspaper. It was dated six months ago, and Ralph recalled the story while looking at the large bold headline—ARLINGTON SEN-TENCED TO LIFE. Robert Arlington had been sentenced to life for first-degree murder. Ralph read the front-page story with renewed interest.

Last Wednesday, without telling his mom, Ralph had placed an advertisement in the local newspaper for a rental property manager. He returned to his office early Monday morning to field the telephone calls from the Sunday ad. His future plans were still incomplete, but he did know that he no longer wanted to deal with renters and spend long hours of inactivity in his office. By end of day, his busiest one in months, he had eliminated all but two applicants.

He called Michelle Barker, a single mom, the next day for a second interview and hired her.

When Ralph talked with her during the first interview, he was pleased with her deportment and believed she would be a good manager based on her prior experience. Being honest, though, the main reason he hired her was for the way she maintained eye contact while talking with him. Her dark brown eyes contrasted to her light blonde hair and seemed to transmit honesty straight from her heart. Ralph met with his new manager several times during the next week to talk about business.

It would be another week before the rest of his plans were in place.

Ralph learned, during his second meeting with Michelle, her car was impounded at a garage because she couldn't pay the repair bill. When he hired her, he didn't know how desperately she needed a job. Her car was impounded at an auto-repair garage, and she had no money for another month's rent where she lived because she had lost her part-time job three weeks before.

Ralph knew none of this when he hired her. He saw a delightful and independent person whom he believed would be a good manager.

During a discussion about specific job requirements, he found out about the car and the rest. She was struggling to get her daughter, Emileigh, to and from school.

With Ralph's help, Michelle got her car back with a much lower bill. That's when the upstairs apartment above his office was presented for her consideration. Michelle was also introduced that same day to Flash, the maintenance man—the one she would be calling to fix any problem with the units. Flash had a truck and moved her few possessions into the apartment.

To repay Ralph for his kindness, she prepared lasagna for him the following Saturday night.

During their meal, he mentioned the newspaper story about Robert Arlington. Michelle remembered following the news accounts of the case. She believed the man was innocent.

They then discussed the man's innocence or guilt. Ralph had reviewed the transcript of the trial and used some of his skills in playing prosecutor. He found Michelle to be quite an interesting opponent. She quickly and clearly expressed her thoughts and opinions.

Driving home, Ralph Fenny knew his next avenue of pursuit. He was going to talk to Robert Arlington.

His conversation with Michelle had been so refreshing that he wanted to learn more about this man who was convicted and sentenced to life in prison. Yes, he would talk to Mr. Arlington, and maybe, just maybe, he would lead an appeal for the man Michelle believed to be innocent.

He would pursue the rule of law first and then consider his belief of innocence or guilt.

CHAPTER TWO

" . . . when I first heard her beautiful voice. "

Ralph was disappointed with himself for not having anticipated the appearance and demeanor of Robert Arlington before he first met him in prison. Although Ralph had seen several pictures of him in the old newspapers, the man before him was noticeably different. He looked much older and emaciated. There was sadness in his eyes that revealed months of depression and futility of hope.

Ralph introduced himself and told Robert about the newspaper his mother had found. He told him about his law practice, his rental units, and that he had just hired someone to manage his rental business.

He later replayed his introductory words and couldn't remember if he had *named* his manager, Michelle. She was becoming much more than a "someone."

The sad-eyed man remained silent. Ralph stopped talking and looked at the defeated man—a man who undoubtedly had once been a strong, cheerful person with many dreams to follow. Robert Arlington only nodded at the beginning of their meeting. He looked down at the table without changing his forlorn expression.

Ralph suddenly closed and locked his briefcase. At the click of the lock, Robert abruptly raised his head and looked at the man who was volunteering to give him hope of a better life. The sound from the briefcase lock must have triggered the dreadful and hopeless feeling associated with closing cell doors. That sound was the essence of the degenerative reality of what the justice system had handed him.

During an instance of eye contact, Ralph saw not only sadness, but also desperation. He saw a man stripped of dignity and denied his rightful place in society. In that instant, Ralph believed in his heart that this man could be innocent. He momentarily remembered how Michelle had argued his innocence. Ralph also believed that for the first time since his incarceration, hope was returning to the defeated man's mind.

During his brief period of talking, Ralph told him about reviewing the court transcripts and conveyed to him that he was convicted on the "best evidence" presented at the trial. The prosecutor presented the "best" and the jury believed. Ralph also told him that an appeal could be possible with *new* evidence. He added that Robert's defense attorney must have also believed the prosecutor because he never mentioned a possible appeal to him.

Until this moment, Robert must have believed new evidence was no more probable than finding the proverbial needle in a haystack. He looked at the closed briefcase as if begging for Ralph to reopen it and reopen his case.

Looking into Robert's eyes, Ralph sensed a hint of cooperation. He then mentally reviewed some of the transcript material.

Robert was convicted for killing his first cousin, Jesse Lynn. The prosecutor had convinced the jury that the criminal act was not only with evil intent, but also premeditated because his girlfriend, Mary, dumped him for Jesse. The prosecutor used an effective courtroom procedure when questioning Mary: "Did you date Robert Arlington?" She answered "Yes." "Did you stop dating Robert and start dating Jesse Lynn?" "Well I . . . it was like . . . "

"Just answer yes or no," barked the prosecutor. A frightened Mary left the witness stand crying. She was concealing a secret that she was sure would be a convicting motive and could be the death of Arlington.

Random details of the transcript were still racing through Ralph's mind when he remembered a scene in Michelle's kitchen during dinner. While standing, she placed her foot on a chair seat to remove a drop of spilled food from her shoe. The outline of her leg could be seen under her cotton dress.

The scene had paraded through Ralph's memory many times. He also remembered her pretty face, her wit, and her finesse during their lively discussions. And he remembered her soft laughter.

Robert looked at Ralph for a few seconds before speaking.

"I guess you know from the newspapers and transcript that I'm an electrical engineer. Right out of college, I went to work for the power company in Huntington, West Virginia. I lived at home and worked most all the time. During the two years with the power company, before meeting Mary, I took only three days of vacation. With some urging from a co-worker, I decided to tour all six New England states."

Robert lowered his head and stared at the tape recorder. He was corralling memories that had been flung from his once happy consciousness and buried in the gloomiest catacomb of his mind—memories that he never expected to retrieve.

Robert looked up and focused his eyes on the wall behind Ralph. While still looking at the wall, Ralph heard mellow, dreamy words.

"It was Friday, August the 15th 1997, when I met Mary Bly O'Day. But I need to back up three weeks to Friday, July the 25th, when I first heard her beautiful voice.

"Hello, how may I help you?"

Robert was momentarily mesmerized by the Yankee accent of that soft voice. Just holding the telephone and not answering, he heard "Hello" again—more melodic than before.

"Oh, uh, yes, hello."

For some reason, he couldn't say anymore. The sweet, Yankee voice repeated the request with sincere concern, " How may I help you?"

Robert had called the Vermont Department of Tourism located on State Street in Montpelier. His plans were to fly to Connecticut and then drive through all six states and depart by plane from Vermont. This was the last of six calls. The other five were of a couple minutes duration. He stated his request for travel and vacation information, and after giving his mailing address, was simply informed that the state's vacation packet would be promptly mailed.

This call to Vermont was so different from the other five. He was feeling an unexplained attraction to the beautiful voice that strangled his own vocal cords. After another attempt to state his request, Robert was soon talking comfortably with the intriguing person. Right after his request, he asked if she would recommend some interesting Vermont attractions. With an easy flow of questions and answers between the two strangers, there soon appeared to be a mutual attraction vibrating through the telephone line.

Robert's thoughts wandered as he looked across his office; the New England trip plan was going to be reversed. He would fly to Vermont first and then drive through the other states. In pleasing disbelief, he realized they had talked more than twenty minutes. Her name was Mary. She had just completed her master's degree and was working part-time with the Department of Tourism. She was living at home with her mother. He tried to remember other parts of the conversation—but couldn't because his mind was filled with a pleasant, mellow blank. He went to the restroom and combed his hair and checked his teeth as if Mary was soon going to appear before him. He did remember she had commented near the end of the conversation that she had never talked this long to anyone while at work.

Back at his desk, still lost in his thoughts, Robert closed his eyes and tried to concentrate on what he could recall. He didn't believe she was married since she was living at home with her mother. Was she engaged? Umm, maybe—he had no firm basis for yes or no. Well anyway, he had definitely decided to visit 134 State Street in Montpelier, Vermont. And just maybe, he could meet Mary. "Well now," he thought, " I don't even know her last name."

Three Weeks Later ☺

It was almost eleven a.m. when Robert walked into the state tourism office building in Montpelier. He was more nervous than when in speech class when in college. Ten minutes sitting in the car had not calmed him. He looked around the room and saw a young woman seated at a desk forward of the other desks. She was talking on the telephone with her back to him. Long auburn hair and a mint green blouse were his initial image of this woman. She turned to reveal her profile. In this side view, he could see that her facial features were beautiful.

Robert stood frozen just a few steps inside the room. When they looked directly at each other, he saw even more beauty. Then a smile lifted and enhanced her cheeks, complete with two small dimples. He just knew she was Mary. Before collapsing, he walked toward her with a surprising boldness. He struggled to get words out of his dry mouth as he looked at the most beautiful woman he had ever seen.

"Hel . . . hello Mary."

"Well hello to you."

She said those four words with a hint of surprise from hearing her name.

Robert could feel the boldness ebbing. He knew some words must come fast.

"We talked on the tele . . . telephone." In a flash, he realized how stupid that must have sounded—she talked all the time on the phone. "We talked about vacation—I called *you*."

He thought, "O boy, this is really stupid. She wouldn't have called me. Her job is to *receive* calls."

Mary didn't speak. She just looked up at his handsome, suntanned face and at his black, wavy hair. She was having her own problems, and wasn't even sure he was talking. Suddenly, she sensed that she was staring. Even so, she kept eye contact and sheepishly smiled. At the same time, Robert sensed that he too was staring, but couldn't do anything about it until she smiled. That impish expression on her creamy face propelled him to speak while still looking into her dark brown eyes under neatly arched eyebrows.

"It was three weeks ago. I'm Robert Arlington. I'm from . . . "

Mary jumped up, with her hand near her mouth, beaming with a smile of comprehension, "Arlington, oh yes, you're from Vir, no, West Virginia." And in the same breath, "You're visiting all New England states starting in Connecticut, and Vermont is your last one. See, I remembered. Did you enjoy the other states?"

Robert's mouth was partially open as he was almost looking directly into her sparkling eyes. Without hesitation he exclaimed, "You're tall!"

He thought she had to be nearly six feet.

Mary nodded as Robert answered her question.

"No." He paused and continued, "Well, I changed my itinerary. I haven't been to the other states. I decided to see Vermont first and then leave from Connecticut.

Mary looked at him, expressionless. Robert took a deep breath.

"I wanted to meet you first and thank you for being so helpful when we talked on the phone." He stopped and lowered his head.

Mary tilted her head and changed her blank expression to one of puzzlement. She was trying to remember how she had helped him during the phone conversation. She had mailed him a standard vacation packet, which was no different from other states' packets. "So how did I help?" She wondered.

Robert could hardly believe the weakness in his legs and how warm he was. He knew his request must be delivered quickly. After another deep breath, "Mary."

He paused, looking at her as if she were an angel. "She must be an angel," he thought while letting her radiance fill his heart with a peace that was both disturbing and comforting. As he continued looking, he thought, "How beautiful." Her face seemed to glow with an air of innocence. Yes, she was standing tall in his eyes. Robert tried again.

"Mary, could I . . . could I take you to lunch . . . today? I want to . . . " He saw a quick change of expression on her and knew to stop talking.

Her face changed from glowing to a mild configuration of shock. Mary was indeed shocked. A stranger wanted to take her out of this room and possibly drive her away in a car. Sure, he seemed nice and he was handsome. She then remembered from their phone conversation that he was a Sunday school teacher. She looked at his suntanned hands and clean fingernails. Her eyes then focused on some papers on her desk. She had never dated much. Her priority during high school and college had been studying. She had been comfortable spending most of her time in the books and only dated with other couples. She was now getting warm.

"This man," she thought, "Who I have known only a few minutes, wants a date with me. Sure, we talked on the phone—but I never expected to ever see him." With a quick movement, Mary looked into his blue eyes, which seemed to reflect a twinkle of disappointment. She didn't know how long it had been since he asked her to have lunch with him. Robert was about to say something else to let her know that he was asking with only honorable intentions. Before he could put together some words, Mary leaned over closer to him and whispered, "Just a minute . . . "

As she walked to the back of the room, he thought, "Gee! How beautiful she is." Earlier, he had wanted to sit down, and now he did before totally collapsing. Robert had only breathed a few times when Mary returned with an older lady. They were both smiling. He thought, "Mary's smile is different—more with her eyes—more relaxed." She would have disputed Robert's assessment had she known what he was thinking. She had just made an unprecedented decision to have lunch with a stranger and was still shaking inside. But he couldn't have known that by the way she lyrically introduced her coworker.

"Arlington, this is Abby Brooks. She will cover for me while we have lunch together."

"So nice to meet you Ms. Brooks . . . "

"It's a pleasure to meet you—and my name is Abby."

"Okay, Abby."

"He's Robert Arlington from West Virginia. We're friends, and he stopped by to see me. We have a lot to talk about."

Robert could hardly believe what he was hearing. Mary was so upbeat and eager to go.

"Ready Arlington?"

All he could do was nod in the affirmative after he got his mouth to close.

Abby called out after they had taken a few steps from the desk, "Have you two known each other long?"

Robert had recovered some and quickly picked up Mary's lead—"We haven't talked for almost a month. We have a lot of catching up to do."

In the car, Mary seemed tense and only spoke to give directions. Robert didn't press for conversation. He was so thankful to be sitting beside her and didn't want to upset his good fortune. After they were seated in the restaurant, she was noticeably more relaxed as they looked at each other across the table. Both were adjusting to their newfound companionship. Robert spoke first.

"Mary, it's so wonderful to be here with you. After we talked on the phone, I knew my plans would be changed. I wanted to hurry up here and meet you and . . . " He paused. "And have lunch with you."

"Well here we are old friend." She emphasized old, and both laughed as if they really were old friends.

The waitress suddenly appeared and remarked, "Well, are we happy today?"

Between some giggling, each ordered a club sandwich and a salad. Robert smiled a lot, particularly when he was content and happy. To Mary, his smiling, clear blue eyes seemed to sparkle and transmit his honest character. She looked especially radiant to him as her smile warmed his heart like he had never known before.

After this little assessment period, Robert asked her, "So have you found a job yet?"

"Not yet."

They talked a little more about job seeking and where she attended college before Robert suddenly put up his hand and declared, "Wait a minute!"

Mary was a little startled, and displeasure was clearly seen on her face that soon changed to a sweet smile as she responded to Robert's wide smile.

"Now I don't know your major, but bet I can guess."

"Who have you been talking to?"

"No one, just bet I can. See that coconut cream pie over there?" Mary nodded.

"Okay, I guess right and you pay for our pie."

Quickly, she replied, "Okay smart guy, you're on."

Robert mentioned several professions, and would give some reason for it not being her major. After a minute or so, he paused for a rather long time. His eyes were closed as he repeated "Art or music, art or music—um—let's see—music, music." Then he blurted, "English—you're an English major, not literature but grammar or composition." He pointed his finger at his astonished friend and declared, "That's it—English."

Mary almost screamed, "How did you know? Who have you been talking to?"

Robert tilted back his head and twisted his face into a quirky grin. "Oh I'm just good. My grandfather taught me all about horses and how to discern their worth and—"

Mary quickly and loudly interjected, "Now wait a minute—I am not a horse!" They blankly looked at each other for an instant before exploding with uncontrollable laughter.

After a few seconds, Robert was wiping tears with one hand and waving for the waitress with the other. When standing by the table, she just rolled her eyes. Robert finally ordered the pie and quickly added—ending in a falsetto tone, "On a separate ticket."

After a few bites, Robert announced, "Yum, this is the best coconut cream pie I have ever tasted—mmm, especially good."

Mary looked straight at him sternly. The smirk left his face. "You haven't tasted *my* pie."

Robert wanted to say, "Sure would like to." But having lunch with her was all he could expect. Mary realized she was extending an invitation but didn't know what to say next. Robert rescued her.

"It's not really that good. I would love to sample your pie." He lowered his head looking at the half-eaten pie. Mary surprised herself when her thoughts became audible. "Guess we should go?"

Robert felt a wave of sadness because their time together was coming to an end. Mary also experienced a twinge of sadness, as the closure of their time together was imminent. She had enjoyed being with this interesting guy.

There was little talking on the return trip to the office. After parking, Robert looked at Mary with melancholy dripping from his long face. She mimicked his expression as they briefly glanced at each other. Neither made a move to exit the car. Just before the silence could have been embarrassing, Robert spoke in a regrettable tone.

"You know, I feel bad about you paying for the pie." Before Mary could reply, he continued, "I would . . . like to . . . do you think I could repay you? Could I take you to dinner tonight?"

Before Mary could answer, she let her tense body relax and had visions of a few more hours with this wonderful man who was now a friend—no longer a stranger. After what Robert thought were minutes, she slowly nodded her head up and down. Turning and looking fully into Robert's begging eyes, Mary Bly O'Day whispered, "Yes, I would like that."

Ralph turned off the tape recorder.

"Well Robert, I'm anxious to meet Mary. She sounds like a wonderful person."

"Yes, she's more than wonderful. It was love at first sight." He thoughtfully paused before continuing.

"There was a lonely period after she met my first cousin, Jesse Lynn, but that actually turned out to be a good thing for us . . . until I ended up in this place."

After a brief discussion about their next meeting, Ralph walked out of the prison into bright sunlight. He was thinking that Robert and Mary's meeting must have been providential, and then this terrible thing happened to them. He was hooked on Robert's story. What possibly could have happened? How could Mary dump Robert for Jesse?

Did Robert, in fact, kill Jesse in a fit of rage? And what did he mean "that actually turned out to be a good thing?"

CHAPTER THREE

. . . nothing else mattered

Just last week, Abby told Mary about a nice new restaurant. It had been agreed that Mary would make dinner reservations. When she called Robert at the motel, he was lying on the bed staring at the ceiling and thinking about the past few hours.

"Was Mary only a mirage? Was her image just refracted light from a distant angel?"

Robert suddenly rolled his head to look out the window. With his eyes squinted, he was remembering the short time he had been with her. Then, with his eyes closed, he unhappily realized that he had not touched her—not even a hand or arm. He sadly thought she might have been a mirage, but they had talked and laughed." Robert was pinching his arm when the phone rang. He had never heard a louder ring.

Mary was lying on her bed when she called the motel. She had made reservations over thirty minutes before and had since been lying on her back staring at the ceiling. She was remembering the short time with Robert that somehow seemed like days. She smiled as her thoughts lingered on the scene about the horse and his grandfather. Really just minutes together, but the intensity and the emotional backlash of being with this wonderful person were confusing her orderly mind. The network of nerves in her brain was buzzing as her thoughts and feelings were often colliding. Finally, with a dreamy smile, she realized they were going to have dinner together.

After the short telephone conversation, Robert jumped off the bed and headed toward the door. Mary had told him that casual clothes were prohibited at the restaurant and had apologetically asked if that was okay. He couldn't tell her his original plans did not include any fancy restaurants. Out the door he flew to buy a suit and a shirt and a tie and even shoes. This would be a small price to pay to be with her again.

Mary had given good directions, and Robert had no problem finding her house. He was early, so drove around the block two times before knocking on the door five minutes before the agreed time. He had always tried to be early for appointments.

When the door opened, Robert's eyes saw Mary's mother, Maureen O'Day. She was also tall, and her mature beauty didn't surprise him. He just knew Mary's mother would be beautiful. Maureen cautiously looked at the young man Mary had excitingly described as "something wonderful." After her brief inspection, Robert was invited inside. Maybe it was his smile or his new suit, but Maureen was soon feeling comfortable in his presence. Only a few boys and men had been invited to wait in Maureen's front room to take her daughter out on a date. Whether by design or necessity, it would be five minutes before she appeared.

Robert smoothly transitioned his few introductory remarks into explaining why he was here to take Mary out for dinner. He told her about the earlier phone call and the coconut crème pie. Maureen had already heard the story from Mary. During their conversation, he was observing her gorgeous hair. It was redder than Mary's auburn shade. Maureen didn't show any noticeable displeasure listening to Arlington. She was, however, wondering if this guy had honorable intentions or if he was the classical traveling salesman type. Before she could conclude exactly what she thought about his character, a radiant Mary appeared on the stairs.

Robert wasn't truly ready for the revelation that zipped from his sight to his brain and then settled in his heart. Mary was standing on the third step up the stairs when he first saw her. She was wearing a long, black dress with wide shoulder straps. The top was semi-low and straight across. A small window above the stair landing backlighted this slender, curvy angel. The illumination behind her was like a Hollywood technique to enhance the star of the show. She had momentarily stopped on the third step as if waiting for permission to stand with her mother and the man who was starting to change her perspective on life.

When Robert started breathing again, he walked toward her. As she stepped onto the living room floor, he remembered his earlier thoughts about not touching her. He wanted to take her in his arms and dance around the room—with or without music. Instead, he extended his clammy hand, only touching her fingertips as if fearing an electrical shock. When his fingertips did brush hers, nerve endings tingled and capillaries seemed ready to explode. It was a feeling he had never experienced before. After a few heartbeats, he walked his fingers up hers and gently clasped her hand. He would never forget the warmth and softness of Mary's hand. They were looking deeply into each other's eyes when he placed his left hand over their two right hands as if to insulate the magic that was circulating through them. When Maureen cleared her throat, Robert was looking at Mary's half smile that seemed to be asking, "Do I look alright?"

As they walked past Maureen, she didn't or couldn't say anything. Her smile, beaming with a Mother's pride, was her blessing for the trembling couple to exit the room.

In the car, the trembling changed to numbness that soon changed back again to a shaky feeling for Arlington. In a forced mood change, he gladly accepted his good fortune of being close to this beautiful person. But as before in the car, conversation focused on directions to the restaurant. Both were overflowing with emotions unparalleled in their lives. Their hearts were silently rejoicing in the sweetness of being together again and also dreading the bitterness when they would have to again part. "What a true oxymoron." Mary thought.

Neither knew what was going to happen in the next few hours. Mary didn't know she would soon experience a soul-stirring event that would change her life forever. When parked at the restaurant, they had mellowed some, and both seemed ready to enjoy being in each other's company.

When Mary looked at the menu, she cried, "Oh Arlington! Look at these prices! Oh, I'm so sorry. I should have asked Abby."

Robert glanced at the menu and then spoke in soothing words. "Now, now don't worry—I'm on vacation. I'm happy to take you to this fine restaurant."

Mary looked over the menu with a hint of embarrassment in her eyes, and whispered regretfully, "I'm really sorry."

The waiter was asking for their order as Robert waved his hand at Mary indicating it was okay. As he looked at Mary over the menu, he had never seen a more beautiful picture in his life. She was begging forgiveness with her dark brown eyes. He was so honored to be with her that the fifty or sixty dollars would not deter the joy bouncing around in his heart.

After they ordered, Mary said, "Oh Arlington, I feel so stupid."

"What do you mean?"

"Do you know about the New England Culinary Institute?"

Wondering why this would be connected to her feeling stupid, he bluntly replied, "No. Why?"

Mary looked like she was going to cry.

"Oh I feel so bad. It's a school to train chefs. They have their own restaurants that have the best food and . . . "

Mary lowered her head looking at the flowers on the table. Without looking up she forced out some explanatory words, "Right here in Montpelier. We passed one on the way here—The Chef's Table on Main Street. When Mary looked up, Robert's expression indicated he was trying to understand why she was so upset. Apologetically, Mary continued, "At The Chef's Table, they have student chefs in training preparing delicious meals and the cost is half these prices."

Robert was aware of Mary's sincerity and concern about the prices, but the cost of dinner was far from his concern at this moment. When they met earlier, her hair was brushing her shoulders. Tonight, it was pinned up with some dangling wisps. Since his first sight of her tonight standing on the stairs, he had been admiring her long slender neck and her curves accented by her black dress.

These two young people, who were desperately groping for direction with their new relationship, just looked at each other for a few lovely seconds. Robert was feasting on the beauty of an angel with a perfectly proportioned neck. Mary thought

Robert looked handsome in his suit and tie. The jacket fit snugly around his broad shoulders and his shirt and tie were nice complements. This was racing in her mind as she admired his suntanned, strong-jawed face. But at lunch, she had also liked his pocket tee and Dockers, which prompted her to say, "I think I'm going to cry." Not waiting for a response, she continued with a strained effort to deliver her words.

"There is no formal dress code at The Chef's Table. Just look at us."

"I like what I see."

Robert almost said, "I needed a new suit." Instead, he pulled on his lapel and continued, "I don't mind. At home, I don't wear a suit often." It was his left hand tugging on his lapel.

Mary's expression slowly changed from melancholy to a scant smile. Then her head and shoulders twitched a few times as her smile widened. She lowered her head while covering her mouth with her hand. When she looked up at Arlington, the puzzled look on his face propelled her into full laughter. Robert noticed her eyes glistened—they were awash with funny-time tears. She tried to constrain herself from laughing while trying to speak. All she could manage was a finger pointing generally in his direction. Then the twitching became shaking and her face changed from a pink blush to blood red. In a quick movement, both hands covered her mouth.

When Robert tugged on his lapel, Mary saw a white sticker on the cuff of his new suit jacket. It wasn't large, but still a signal contrast to the dark gray fabric. Robert was befuddled at her emotional outburst. Her mirthful expression, without explanation, was starting to make him wonder if he was the origin of her glee.

Finally with reserve strength from somewhere deep within her shaking body, she managed to speak. "Cuff! On your cuff."

Robert was still perplexed as he looked at his right cuff. When he raised his eyes, Mary was wiping tears. He then looked at his left cuff. The realization was instant. He looked up at the beautiful girl across the table. Her makeup was flawless minutes before. Now, still recovering from her spasms of uncontrollable laughter, dark rivulets of mascara were meandering down her flushed face.

He pleaded, "What was I to do? I didn't bring a suit, and I didn't have much time."

Mary's appearance suddenly changed from a happy smiling face to one with a sullen expression complete with a full-face frown. Her tears were still flowing but were now hot and burning. Robert observed the change and was about to offer consoling words when Mary slowly shook her head and squeaked a mousy reply.

"Oh Robert, I feel so bad. I caused you to buy a new suit." She paused as more tears and dark rivulets trickled down her cheek.

Robert sensed the depth of her regret and wanted to change her back to the happy Mary before the bitter tears and frown. He got up from his chair and stood beside her. She tilted her head back with a wondering expression on her smudged face.

"Do the bottom of my new suit pants look okay?"

Mary wiped more tears as she lowered her head. "Well, maybe the crease is a bit puffy, but I guess they look okay."

As Robert was bending over, he flatly stated that the store couldn't hem them until tomorrow. He rolled up a pant leg while announcing, "See! I fixed it myself. See?—Duct tape."

Mary's bleary eyes did indeed see the familiar silver-gray duct tape on the inside of his pant leg. He had turned the material inward and simply applied the tape along the raw edge. The next thing she saw was his impish grin. He saw her sad countenance slowly change to one that included tight thin lips and eyelids that were partially closed to mere slits. He quickly exclaimed, "My grandfather told me, 'sometimes you have to improvise.'"

Mary exploded first, and then they both laughed and laughed losing track of time. Robert noticed the waiter was looking in their direction several times. Mary actually sputtered as she spoke.

"Oh Arlington, I have never laughed this much. Never—never."

On the third try, she asked if his shoes were also new. Robert conveyed his answer with a nod. He then asked if she liked his new shirt and tie. After another season of laughing, it finally happened—Mary saw the telltale smudges on her napkin. She needed to fix her face. Laughing was over for now.

Robert was transfixed when she approached the table, all the rivulets of mascara were gone and her composure was nearly back to normal. Barely breathing, he watched her glide toward him with a carriage befitting a princess. He couldn't move to assist seating her. He could only gaze at this tall, beautiful girl with burnished auburn hair framing her radiant face. He was also peering beneath surface beauty and thinking of intrinsic qualities more valuable than outward beauty of the earth angel before him.

The time of gaiety wasn't the reason for what happened next. It was, however, a necessary prerequisite for a more profound emotion that was circling Robert Lynn Arlington and Mary Bly O'Day. They both seemed to sense something significant was coming. Maybe a grand judicial figure larger than the room was going to make a momentous proclamation. During the past few mellow moments, their thoughts and feelings had crystallized to a clarity that was reflected in their solemn eyes. The merriment of the past minutes was securely filed in the Archives of Romance—titled, "Getting to Know You."

After Mary was seated, her smile seemed to be apologizing to Robert for the new suit and duct tape episode. Her oval face with accented cheeks was again flawlessly stunning. For a sweet twist of time, they looked deeply at each other. Words would have been extraneous during this precious instant when they both sensed the full significance of being together tonight. Nothing else mattered in their respective worlds at this breathless tick of time. All previous tethered warranted priorities were severed and set free because nothing else mattered beyond being together at this moment. This moment, when a thousand dreams tumbled within Robert's racing heart. This moment, when a like number of hopeful thoughts churned in Mary's heart until it ached. Nothing else mattered to two young people as they looked at each other unabashedly but also lost in a dimension compassed with a magic ardor.

Robert slowly extended his hand. Without hesitation, Mary's hand effortlessly met his big hand at the middle of the table. While they maintained eye contact, a two-way consoling current of affection flowed through their clasped hands. Robert's grandfather would often consummate an agreement with a handshake. The unspoken pact transmitted between these moist hands was no less binding in agreeing they were falling in love.

Robert was thinking about her compassion and her remorse for the new suit. Mary was thinking of his monetary sacrifice to please her. She felt honored to be in his company. Robert was feeling a joyous exhilaration beyond any previous moment in his life. To be in her presence was a gift he didn't deserve. But he considered it fate and would gladly accept it. Mary's greatest moment of joy tonight, however, was yet to surround her. Robert thought, "If the waiter was looking now, he would surely see a glow emanating from our hands as shy inhibitions melt like iron ore in a crucible."

Without words, they both knew it was time to leave this fancy restaurant. They would be leaving behind a paragraph

in their life that would be the prelude for a new chapter. Both perceived they were being steered by hands of fate and neither objected. Simultaneously they arose from the table. Walking to the car, Mary was experiencing an enhanced level of emotional bliss. She had always planned next steps in her life, but for the moment, her immediate future was mystically without concern. Her high school and college years flashed through her fuzzy mind. She had conscientiously studied and achieved great academic honors of high school valedictorian and third in her college class. Oh yes, she had maintained a disciplined life. But during this walk to the car, she was seemingly floating without full control of her faculties that had always before successfully guided the order of her life. Holding hands as they walked across the parking lot, two young innocent people were falling in love. Neither was fully prepared for what was soon to happen in the car.

Ralph was away from home three days. He called Michelle thirty minutes after his arrival. He apologized for the late hour and they talked a little about rental units.

The main reason for his call, however, was that he had so much to tell her about his interview with Robert Arlington. Michelle suggested they have a business dinner meeting at her apartment the next evening.

Ralph Fenny looked critically at himself while shaving. He didn't consider himself handsome. But he did think his thick brown curly hair set him a bit above the ordinary. He knew his blue eyes were bright, and others surely must see honest, good intentions deep in them. He remembered Robert Arlington's sad blue eyes, so full of resentment and hopelessness.

By the end of their second meeting, Arlington had changed to a completely different person. Ralph had asked him to tell everything about Mary O'Day. Ralph explained that he needed to know when, how, and why he became acquainted with Mary. He also emphasized that Robert must tell everything he knew about Jesse Lynn.

Ralph was bubbling with all he had learned from Arlington. At the beginning he told Robert that his deposition would be shared with Michelle. He felt her discerning mind could help in formulating the appeal format.

Each time he thought of Michelle, an unfamiliar feeling would sail through his mind. He had never dated much and had never been seriously attracted to anyone until now. Ralph was an only child still living with his Mother when he first met Michelle—he guessed his heart just flipped. His world, until then, had been his mother and his education. He had worked hard at college and didn't have much time for dating. Actually, he didn't make much time for that type of extra curricular activity. There had been some group gatherings where he was with a girl, but not a real date. Now after meeting Michelle, his whole perspective on life had changed.

CHAPTER FOUR

"Do you believe in angels?"

"Well, what do you think so far?"

Michelle looked up at Ralph. Her eyes were moistened—near to overflowing. She had intently listened as Robert and Mary were falling in love. Her thoughts were too intense to immediately answer. She was remembering a few years before when she met Mark Barker. He had transferred to her high school in the tenth grade. They were both sixteen. She was fighting old guilt feelings that were now producing some tears of shame in her dark brown eyes.

Mark was a handsome football player and she was so honored when he picked her. She was young and innocent and didn't know the male tendency to charm and flatter during their conquest of virgins. She knew later that her attraction to him was physical and that her yielding was human. Before Emileigh was born, Michelle accepted Jesus as her personal savior and knew she was forgiven of her sins with Mark. But it was hard to quell the lingering memories of reproach that were now filtering through her sterling convictions.

"Michelle, what do you think about Robert and Mary? Without waiting any longer for a reply, "I think they were predestined to meet and . . . " Ralph stopped when he noticed tears actually streaming down her face.

Her best intentions to answer him totally collapsed when she heard him say—predestined. In a fleeting moment of anger, she wondered if she and Mark were meant to meet. But she quickly recovered from defying God's will in her life when she thought of Emileigh. She answered Ralph with acclamation.

"Yes!"

Puzzled, he looked at the attractive brown-eyed blonde who was trying to smile. And he was trying to remember just what he asked that would oblige such a resounding "Yes."

"Yes Ralph, I also believe they were brought together by winds of destiny. I heard every word as their relationship sweetly migrated from stranger to friend and tooo . . . "

Her voice became inaudible with the long "os" as she slowly lowered her head. Before he could discern her platform of thoughts, he saw her big, brown eyes looking up at him. At first, begging or pleading flashed through his mind. Then he saw a sheen of honesty reflected in her eyes as she spoke.

"Ralph." Hesitating before repeating his name—"Ralph, I've done some things in my life that I'm not a bit proud of."

Even though they had only known each other for a few weeks, and had not been together but a few hours, she comfortably continued.

"I dated a football player while I was a sophomore in high school." Michelle looked out the window before resuming eye contact with Ralph. "When Robert said they weren't prepared for what happened when they returned to the car—what do you think happened?"

Ralph's expression transmitted that he was in the search mode. Still maintaining eye contact, he finally answered, "I don't know. I have, however, formed an opinion about their character but will say that amorous temptation is a mighty force."

Michelle looked out the window again before speaking. "Mark and I . . . Mark Barker and I dined at a restaurant one evening. It wasn't a fancy one like Robert described. Afterwards, we too walked across a parking lot to his car. We repeated this routine often. We were both sixteen."

In an emotional discourse, she conveyed to Ralph that after becoming pregnant, she was ashamed of her irresponsible actions. But she had accepted Jesus as her personal Savior before Emileigh was born and had survived to this day because of His forgiving love and because of His concern for her well being. At this junction of what Ralph deemed a confession, she covered her face with both hands. For a few seconds, she cried. Ralph didn't know it at the time, but she was crying tears of joy. She was remembering the many times in her short life she had experienced fear, uncertainties, hopelessness, and even hunger. Glory-spiked tears were filling her hands as she recalled how the Lord had lifted her spirits and provided her needs during each low time in her Christian life. Like right now—she had a good job with a good place to live. A few weeks ago, she was nearly as low as she had ever been.

In a flash, she remembered the Sunday night church service when she accepted Jesus. A lady she didn't know asked her, "If you died tonight would you go to Heaven?" In her heart she knew the answer was no. They went to the altar and the lady helped her pray the sinner's prayer. "Dear Lord, I am a sinner. I ask you to forgive me and make me one of your own. I believe you died for my sins and were buried and arose from the grave and you are now in Heaven where I will be some day."

Michelle Barker regained a semblance of composure before returning her attention to Ralph. Her face was flushed with a mixture of embarrassment and thanksgiving. Glistening tear stains highlighted the sincerity of her passion for her Savior. During the past few minutes she didn't know how much she had talked or how much she had thought. She didn't expect any pity from Ralph nor did he extend any. He liked her when he first saw her and now he was wondering if he was falling in love with her. He then quickly wondered what his mother would think about him loving a single mom. Michelle looked at Ralph as if to say, "I'm sorry." But without saying anything, she left the room.

They had been sitting in the living room since dinner ended. While Michelle was out of the room, Ralph assessed his thoughts and feelings. His summary was only a fluttering around his heart. Before his confused thoughts could recycle, Michelle melodically called from the kitchen announcing it was time for some tea and lemon pound cake. After Mary's laughter time, she and Robert closed a gap in their relationship. After Michelle's crying time, Ralph was sensing that the space between their true feelings was lessening.

While they were seated again at the small kitchen table, the conversation changed to an incident with one of the renters. Ralph then commented about the good cake and casually mentioned the lateness of the day. He had actually wanted to say something about the beautiful evening with her—maybe he would later. Michelle didn't react in any way to his comment about the late hour. He didn't know it, but she wasn't through with this evening yet.

With no preamble to her forthcoming dialogue, she bluntly stated. "I was six months along when we married. It only lasted ten months—most of them miserable. Emileigh was seven months old when he left. We lived in the basement of Mother's rented house. My dad left when I was four. Mark continued in high school and I finished later. Well anyway, we only lived in the basement for eight months. The worst thing about living in Mom's house was fighting off her men friends before and after I was married. We finally got our own apartment and I was so thrilled with my own place—my castle. It was sparsely furnished, but I was so hopeful of a regular married life. My home life with Mother was a bit dysfunctional. I have never smoked cigarettes or marijuana. I only drank some beer right after meeting Mark. But I do have an addiction. I'm hooked on believing. Believing that someday I will have a house I can make into a home."

Ralph had never loved anyone or anything as much as he loved Michelle at this moment. He wanted to scoop her into his arms and say, "I'll help you make a house a home—I have twenty-three houses. Michelle, pick one, or we can build a new house."

Michelle seemed to be in deep thought before she continued. When she did start talking again, he detected a mystic inflection in her soft voice as she looked directly at him. "Do you believe in angels?"

Ralph was astounded. "What a question," he thought. He had never considered yes or no. He did attend church some. He had spent a good part of his life preparing for his career. This did not leave much time for thoughts or studies about religion or philosophic studies that would explore the validity of angels. He believed himself to be a good person with compassion and concern for others. He had several times struggled with his conscience over a renter who could not pay the rent. He once moved a mother and her baby to another apartment and paid her first month's rent. Yes, his principles were first rate, and he believed in God. He finally decided angels were heavenly beings, but he didn't have any proof of their earthly existence.

Michelle was waiting for an answer.

"Maybe."

"Would you change your 'maybe' to 'yes' if you had proof?"

"Well yes—proof is a significant tool in my profession."

"Mr. Skeptic, would you like to hear a true story about angels? A true story about how angels have helped me survive some really low times in my life?" Not giving him time to answer, she arose from the table and talked while pacing.

"Ralph, I'm an independent person. I've had to be in order to support the two of us. I have overcome some pretty scary obstacles with the Lord's help. I have had some . . . let me say, some varied living conditions. I have been hungry several times but Emileigh hasn't."

She stopped pacing and sat down at the table. With a hint of remorse in her voice, she restarted her story.

"Each time I crawled into the backseat of Mark's car, I was assuming a great responsibly. Now I didn't know that at the time. I was young and may have been rebelling against my mom, but I'm not blaming her. Anyway, Emileigh came along and I have been a responsible mother—she has always had milk and food. If my varied living conditions were measured on a scale from one to ten, I doubt I got to an average three. I have even been a half-jar of peanut butter from a zero."

Thinking of the Mother and baby he had helped relocate, Ralph understood Michelle's prior living conditions. He also understood more about a mother's love. The relocated mom was moving to a less desirable apartment. But as her surroundings were deteriorating, she never wavered in giving enduring attention to her baby.

Michelle was staring at her teacup when she continued. "I survived without any human help for almost two months after Mark left. Mother had left the state with a new male friend. I was alone. I had just turned eighteen."

She raised her head—looking distantly beyond Ralph and quickly spoke. "That was six years ago. Okay, I was totally alone for almost two months. With my last bit of change, I went to the supermarket to buy milk for Emileigh. I did have an old car but with only a quarter-tank of gas. Before getting back into the car, I noticed two sacks of groceries in the backseat. Two large brown sacks that I discovered later were packed full of every imaginable practical type of food item."

More tears trickled down her cheeks. She was remembering how desperately they needed food at that time. Ralph was showing some poignant emotion as he listened. He had never been subjected to wanting or needing situations. He wanted to feel sorry for her but he knew she would not permit it.

If Michelle's motive had been to win Ralph's heart with her sad story—well, she was at the threshold. He looked at her with an endearing hunger that almost propelled him to gather her in his arms and love away all the bad times in her life. Neither moved from their chairs. Michelle's face was dry again as she continued her angel story.

"Included in the groceries were One-A-Day Vitamins and St. Joseph Baby Aspirins." She smiled as if to say, "Can you believe that?" She started pacing again.

"I went back in the store and asked if two sacks of groceries had been reported lost. After ten minutes, I left for home with a glow in my heart that matched how I felt when I accepted Jesus into my life."

Michelle sat back down at the table and slightly lowered her head as if she were beginning a nod to coach Ralph's reply to her forthcoming question.

"Do you *now* believe in angels?"

He was ready for her question and responded like a good lawyer should.

"There's no proof that an angel put the groceries in your car. From what you have told me, no one saw a person or a 'being' place the sacks in your car." He thought, "Where is this going?"

Michelle glanced at Ralph as she arose from the table again. She was walking toward the sink when she suddenly turned around. Sternly and factually, she proclaimed, "Okay, that was part A. Are you ready for part B?"

Feeling trapped, Ralph nodded in the affirmative.

Michelle pointed her finger at him. "First, back to 'A' for a minute. Those two sacks of groceries contained exactly the items a frugal person would buy with a limited amount of money. There was not one extravagant item—no candy, no soft drinks and no cigarettes. There was, however, one bag of animal crackers. I would have bought every item except maybe the vitamins even though I needed them."

With a slight sneer and her head lifted back, "Alright Mr. Skeptic Lawyer man, I rest part 'A' of my case and now call Ms. Michelle Barker to the witness stand." She was smiling and pacing again.

"Can you, Ms. Barker, tell all present that angels do exist on this planet earth?"

Ralph jumped up and nearly shouted. "I OBJECT! Council is leading the witness to make a statement that has not been proven in this . . . "

His voice trailed off and his reactive courtroom expression was replaced with a little smirky grin. Michelle placed her fingertips on her smiling lips as she contemplated her next move. She sat down and continued just above a whisper.

"Four days after the groceries, I heard a knock on the front door. I cautiously opened the door and a nice looking young man introduced himself as Alvin Chapman. He handed me a card as he told me about his advertising company. Emileigh walked in the room while we were talking. She was just over one year old. Now hear what I'm going to say next. Mr. Chapman, a stranger, asked—'How old is Emiliegh?'"

Michelle waited for a reaction—not hearing anything from Ralph, she softy proceeded with her story.

"He then remarked about her beauty. Well now, that didn't hurt my feelings. She didn't have on the latest trendy clothes, but she was always neat and clean. I still get her clothes from Goodwill and sometimes they need a little mending but she always looks nice."

Michelle told how Mr. Chapman asked if she would consent to having Emiliegh's photograph made for a poster. She would be a 'poster child' for some advertising campaign in California, and he would give me money for permitting her to pose. Michelle stared at Ralph until he lowered his eyes. She then pointedly asked, "Do you believe what I've been talking about?"

"Partly—well mostly."

"Do you really believe about the groceries?"

"Yes, because you said they were in your car. Yes, I believe that."

"What about Mr. Chapman?"

"Michelle, I have no reason to disbelieve you. All you have told me is real to you."

"Meaning—not real to you Mr. Lawyer?

Ralph quickly replied, "No! No! I'm sorry—please forgive me. I do believe every word you've said." Nodding his head up and down, "I believe."

"Okay! I was to have Emiliegh to the portrait studio, here in town, the following Monday morning at ten. We walked to church Sunday because I wanted to make sure there would be enough gasoline for the Monday appointment. He told me they had paid as high as twelve hundred dollars for a picture. Rent was due the following Wednesday. I doubt you can know . . . "

She stopped and tightened her face to a frown to check more tears. "I would have been evicted. At that time, I couldn't find a suitable baby sitter in order to look for a job. I'm just twenty-four years old and could write a book about all the different types of jobs I've had. Now mind you, I'm not asking for sympathy. I'm just trying to paint a picture of my situation when Mr. Chapman knocked on my front door. I was in a pretty deep valley at that time."

Ralph totally unexpected Michelle's next move. She extended her hand to him. Like Robert and Mary, he clasped her hand over the middle of the table. Her hand was warm with long slender fingers that snugly wrapped around his shaking hand.

"Ralph." She tightened her lips to stop the quivering. "When we got to the portrait studio, I told the receptionist about our 10:00 a.m. appointment that Mr. Chapman arranged. She said they would be ready for us in ten minutes, and then asked, 'Whom did you say sent you in?' I repeated a Mr. Alvin Chapman. She asked a co-worker if she knew an Alvin Chapman? The girl answered, 'No!' I interjected that he was an advertising representative who contacted me last Friday. The receptionist was visually perplexed. She said, 'You do have an appointment, but I don't know how your name got here. I do the appointment book.' After the posing, I was given a check for one thousand and seven dollars."

Michelle slowly withdrew her hand. Ralph was reluctant to surrender this first bit of intimacy with this beautiful girl. She walked into the front room and Ralph followed her. She turned around as he entered the room. He walked to her with his arms outstretched—she responded in like manner and they embraced without a kiss. Michelle immediately started crying again. Over six years since a man had encircled his arms around her. Over six years of loneliness—the tear gates opened wide. She was limp and would have slipped to the floor except for Ralph's strong arms. "All those years without a man's touch," was mostly her thought. Neither was counting so neither knew how long their arms and hearts were tangled. One thing was sure—Ralph's shoulder was wet from her tears as she cried like a baby. He cried with empathy as he sensed her pent-up stress escaping in the warm tears. When the taut fibers of her inner feelings relaxed, she slowing backed out of his arms and left the room.

She returned a few minutes later with a small white Bible in her hand. She had done some face maintenance and treated Ralph with a sweet smile while motioning for him to sit beside her on the sofa. The sofa was covered with what looked like a bedspread. He had previously surveyed her furniture and was tempted to extend some help, but thought better. She was holding the little Bible with both hands and looked at it as she spoke.

"I've told you that before Emileigh was born, I accepted Jesus as my personal Savior. In my hands, I'm holding God's holy inspired word." Turning to look directly at Ralph, "Now I won't entertain any courtroom procedure concerning the validity of this precious book."

The man beside her heard the tone of her voice and humbly nodded.

"Right after Mark left, I was scared. I had just turned eighteen— Emileigh was thirteen months old. What I'm going to tell you happened a short time before the groceries and Mr. Chapman.

One lonely night after Emileigh was asleep, I was reading this Bible. I had just finished the 23rd Psalm and then turned some pages 'til my eyes focused on the 91st Psalm.

Michelle glanced at Ralph. He was looking at the floor. She opened her Bible and beckoned him.

"Ralph."

He abruptly looked in her direction. "I want to read two verses. You can read the other fourteen later. It is Psalm 91: verses 2 and 11.

> *2: I will say of the Lord, He is my refuge*
> *and my fortress: my God; in him will I trust.*

11: *For he shall give his angels charge*
over thee, to keep thee in all thy ways."

Without looking up, she read verse eleven again.

"11: *For he shall give his angels charge*
over thee, to keep thee in all thy ways."

She closed her Bible and walked into the kitchen. She re-entered the living room after a minute announcing that it was two o'clock. Ralph was still sitting on the sofa with his head down. He was trying to retrieve thoughts and emotions that had been tumbling from his mind to his heart.

In lower than her normal tone, she asked, "Ralph, would you go to church with me tomorrow?" Before he could answer, she corrected herself. "I mean today."

After standing, he smiled while saying, "I would like that."

There was not another embrace. Both were a little off balance. But each knew a firm foundation of friendship was laid tonight, and Ralph knew that angels existed. Not solely from Michelle's stories, but from what was now bouncing around in his heart.

Ralph drove home by rote. His mind was spinning a mile a minute while thoughts and emotions were bumping into each other. Before he parked the car, an undeniable, believable fact spun from his heart and mind. "Yes, yes, angels are real, and tonight I even held one in my arms. She had long shimmering blonde hair and big brown eyes."

As Ralph stepped on the front porch, he was not dreading what his mother was going to say about him getting home so late.

A few miles away on the other side of town, Michelle Barker was already asleep. She went to bed with overflowing peace in her heart and had drifted off to sleep while thanking Jesus for all his blessings.

CHAPTER FIVE

"He taught me how to pray . . .

The following Tuesday at 8:30 a.m., Ralph was meeting with Lester Harris, the Prison Warden. He was sixtyish with close-cut salt and pepper hair. Dark, piercing eyes were deep-set and sheltered with heavy, black brows. Ralph was requesting an extended visitation period with Arlington. Lester Harris had an uncanny ability to discern the character of people and their motives. He stared at Ralph for a rather long time before flatly speaking his only words of the meeting.

"From nine to eleven and then one to four."

Ralph nodded.

Mr. Harris stood up, and Ralph also stood knowing this meeting was over.

55

Robert smiled as he greeted Ralph. It was quite a contrast to their first salutation. For both, a lot of thoughts and feelings had flowed down the river of time since their last meeting. With only skimpy preliminaries, Ralph started the next part of the deposition by placing the tape recorder on the table. It was keyed to repeat Robert's last sentence when he and Mary were walking across the parking lot to the car.

"Two innocent people were falling in love and neither was fully prepared for what was going to happen in the car."

When Robert heard his words he reacted with a satisfying smile. He was ready to share a beautiful event that happened one warm, August night in Montpelier, Vermont.

Once in the car, Robert and Mary sat motionless for a couple of minutes. Both were stabilizing their emotions from the past hour. The laughing time and associated tears in the restaurant were set apart from this timorous moment. The next wave of tears, soon to flow, would be coming from a different spring. Robert spoke first.

"You know, Mary, I can hardly believe that we only met this morning. As I sit here beside you, it seems I've known you for at a least a week."

Mary didn't say anything for what seemed like minutes. Then, factually, with a mellow overtone, "Eleven o'clock a.m., August 15, 1997. It is now around eight and I agree it seems like a week since I first saw you standing in the doorway."

Neither knew the road to falling in love. Both had dated some, but soaring to uncharted regions tonight was an unread chapter in their lives. Nevertheless, when they finally smiled at each other, they must have been entertaining such thoughts. They had gone from strangers to friends on a fast track. Now, Robert was at a loss as to what to do next. He knew Mary cared for him, but just what to do or say was making him nervous. He could start the car or he could take her hand or he could say, "I love you, I love you." Before another alternative registered, he remembered a joke that seemed to personify his predicament.

"Mary, want to hear a joke about a boy and his red wagon?"

The parking lot lights made it bright enough in the car for him to see her blank expression as she answered.

"I guess."

"Okay, a little boy had a red wagon and a goat. He hitched the goat to the wagon and started down the road. He soon saw a little girl playmate and asked if she wanted to ride in his wagon? She said, 'No!' The little boy said, 'Nit up doat.' and moved on down the road. This was repeated several times until a little girl got in the wagon. The perplexed little boy asked, 'What I do now doat?'"

Mary didn't smile. Robert was so disgusted with himself for telling that stupid joke. What a way to end a beautiful day. If Mary was surprised or embarrassed about the joke, she didn't show it. Her drained expression was replaced with a semblance of seriousness. She was without direction as much or more than Arlington. Regardless of what they were about to say, they were already marching across the bridge of love to that magic land of romance. Their hearts were seemingly beating with a cadence directed by a force greater than any of their inner strengths, one that would help them to emerge from this bewildering lull in their conversation.

Robert was ready to start the car and drive away from the black hole he was slipping into, when a flash of inspiration filled his being.

"Mary?"

She waited a few heartbeats to modulate her erratic breathing before meekly answering. "Yes."

"Do you remember your grandparents?"

She paused before replying. "Yes and no—I remember Pa Pa Shannon and Ma Ma Colleen McClanahan only from their annual visits. They moved to Austin, Texas in 1976 when I was one year old, and they would come to Vermont for Thanksgiving and stay two weeks. We would also have a Christmas dinner before they left. I have some memories but not necessarily ones I cherish. We didn't really do that much together; and besides, I don't remember anything before four or five."

Mary paused and turned to look through the windshield. With a touch of sadness in her voice, she continued.

"My O'Day grandparents lived and passed away in Ireland. Dad was the youngest of ten children. He came to America in 1970 when he was thirty and married Mother in 1974. No, I hardly know anything about them. Dad didn't talk much about them or his life in Ireland."

In a manner of condolence, Robert asked if her Dad died after a long illness. Mary didn't immediately answer. He added to his question.

"Didn't you tell me he died last year?"

Mary tightened her lips and arduously answered.

"No, it wasn't from a long illness, and yes it was last year. It was sudden and quite unnecessary. He was only fifty-six." She paused again. "It occurred in a pub when two younger men used beer bottles in a fight."

Robert felt so bad for prying. Not once did she use the word "died." In a most apologetic and humble manner he continued, "Mary, I'm so sorry—"

She interrupted, "That's okay, we're big people. Life is full of bumps and curves. I've been able to manage the bumps—it's the curves that scare me. When a speeding event, like today, exceeds the sensibility of controlled living, it's a straight-line fly-away tangent to the curve."

Robert knew the root of that comment. This conversation may have seemed unromantic, but each had a substantial amount of residual tingle coursing through their veins to read the road signs. He also had experienced bumps on his road of life, and he also knew they were speeding to a curve of unknown magnitude. That was a really neat metaphor. He was proud of Mary. Admiration aside, his turn was next. He didn't know if his question about grandparents was from divine prompting or plucked from the air. Nevertheless, he needed to continue.

"I've already told you some about Pa Pa Lynn. I still miss him every day. He died in an automobile accident. Ma Ma Bertha Ruth received a broken leg but is okay now." Robert did not wait for any comment, "My Gramps Arlington, James Robert, is seventy-two and lives near Savanna, Georgia. Granny Ruth Marie is seventy. Oh, I should add that they live together. Like your grandparents, I have never been with them much. They met in 1945, when Gramps was in the Navy, and married in 1946. Granny Ruth is from South Carolina and they have lived there since their marriage. I see them two or three times a year. There has never been any real closeness—respect, yes, but no fond memories like with Pa Pa Lynn."

Robert was still much aware that Mary was only three feet from him. They both had shifted and were nearly facing each other. He had started this grandparent thing and was going to finish it. He didn't read any objection on Mary's face, so he continued.

"Now, with Pa Pa Lynn it's a different story. I really admired him. Maybe it was from so much time with him. I would spend entire summers on the farm. He taught me so many things."

Robert suddenly stopped talking. He was nervous and realized he was talking fast and in short sentences. He took a deep breath and smiled as he said, "He taught me about horses—yes, I know a lot about horses."

Mary returned his smile. She was, apparently, becoming more comfortable. Maybe the inevitable curve could be negotiated without a regrettable "fly away." Robert's thoughts were slowing, and he was also feeling more comfortable. In slow, measured words, he again smiled as he broke the silence with, "Knots. He taught me how to tie twelve different knots. Did I say he was in the Navy?"

Mary nodded. Robert checked again for any signs of boredom. Detecting none, he hurried on with his list of things that made Pa Pa Lynn so special to him.

"Gardening—gardening was maybe his favorite activity. He raised a multitude of vegetables and berries and fruits and took a lot of his time explaining to me why 'this' and 'that' was done a certain way. And during our long hours together, I observed his compassion and kindness extended to people and animals and even to plants. Guess it would be tender loving care for plants. He raised hay for the horses and cows. I will never forget the many times we had to hurry to get the hay into the barn before it rained. But with all the work, we still had time to go fishing a lot. He used to say, 'God intended man to fish a lot because the earth has so much water.' I don't think that was God's original statement."

At this juncture in the concourse of the day's events and emotions, a frown showed on his face as he seemed to ratchet down from the enthusiastic praise of his Pa Pa. He was beginning to believe that talking about grandparents was more stupid than the goat joke. Mary was not asking any questions nor were there any outward signs of enjoyment with his 'down on the farm' narrative. He didn't directly check Mary's temperament since he was again staring at the steering wheel. He was battling with a burning desire to tell her one more lesson he had learned from his mentor. The time with Mary had been a thousand times more beautiful than he had ever expected when their eyes first met. But in the next minute, all the joy in his heart, along with all the unbounded love that could be shared with Mary, was going on the line. He was going to take a less traveled road.

"Mary . . . Mary, I guess the most important thing I learned from Pa Pa was . . . " Robert abruptly stopped and took a deep breath.

"But first let me tell you that I accepted Jesus as my personal savior when I was fourteen." Robert was now looking at Mary. She didn't move an eyelash. He didn't try to guess her thoughts.

"Okay Mary, here's my most precious and valuable lesson and remembrance of Pa Pa Lynn." Slowly and reverently he spoke just above a whisper. "He taught me how to pray. It may not seem like much to some people, but I believe prayer is the most important part of Christian living. Now I didn't know this when I was a young Christian at fourteen. I guess that's why he taught me to pray."

Robert made an attempt to comprehend Mary's reaction to his last statement about prayer. He believed she was in deep thought or maybe deep shock, but she did extend to him a sweet smile. Reinforced by her smile, he conjectured that courage would come to tell her how he learned to pray. Even so, a phrase from his Pa Pa's hillbilly vocabulary came to mind to describe his thinking—a "thousand hundred" thoughts whizzed in and out of his frightened mind. But Robert Arlington, Sunday school teacher from West Virginia, decided to tell this beautiful girl exactly how his Pa Pa Lynn taught him how to pray. He didn't expect any reaction from Mary and was still a little doubtful if this was a proper date theme. But he had already committed to take the less traveled road tonight. He learned at an early age to make decisions and to see them through.

"He said, 'Buddy'—that's what he called me—'I'm going to give you some tips on a good way to learn how to pray. To begin, you humbly bow your head because you are entering into communion with the almighty, supreme God. This is an act of sharing your thoughts and emotions with Him. Now it's fingertips.' I looked at him confused, but he continued, 'Now Buddy, watch what I do and listen to what I say.'" Robert put his left hand just above the steering wheel.

"'Place your thumb on your little finger (Robert did this) and say—Dear Lord, I thank you for your son Jesus. As I believe on him, I know Heaven will some day be my eternal Home. Now Buddy, move your thumb to your ring finger—Thank you Lord for the Bible which is your Holy inspired word. Dear Lord, we know it's the only book we really need to get through this life and then live forever with you in Heaven. Move your thumb to your middle finger—This one is about praying for the unsaved and being an effective witness.'

He said to pray that the unsaved will realize they are lost and will miss Heaven if they continue living without Jesus in their heart. He said, 'Buddy, ask God to help you to live your life so others may see Christ in you. And ask the Lord to give you the desire and strength to witness to sinners. Tell them that Jesus died for their sins, and by believing they will be forgiven and assured life ever after.'"

Robert hesitated before the next finger. "'The forefinger—Pray for the church leaders and church family. Pray for the church to be a lighthouse in the community so the unsaved can be drawn into the House of the Lord.'"

Robert glanced at Mary. She looked at him in a most peculiar way—totally solemn.

"'Now the thumb—Pray for missionaries.' I didn't know any at that time. I do now and call out their names asking the Lord to bless and provide their needs. 'Start over again with the little finger. This would be number six.' He said, 'This part of your prayer is for anything or anyone special. A special need or something you feel strongly about.

Tonight, I would pray that you Mary, my special friend, would find a good job and . . . and find . . . and . . . " Robert didn't finish the sentence. He hurriedly explained the outline for the remaining fingers while looking over the steering wheel through the windshield.

"The next finger—Pray for Government leaders to make decisions pleasing to God's will. The middle finger—Repeat about Jesus. The forefinger—Repeat about the Holy Bible. And the thumb again—close how ever you choose."

Robert had his head bowed as he whispered, "Amen."

When he raised his head and looked at Mary, she was crying. Not a few tears, but really crying. He promptly asked, "Mary are you a Christian?"

Between irregular breathing and sobs, she peeped. "No."

"Would you like to be a Christian?"

She answered more boldly. "Yes."

Robert was sure he was going to pass out. He felt weak and disoriented. His mouth was dry. He had, face to face, led six to Christ—mostly teenagers in his Sunday school class. But Mary, the girl with whom he was falling in love, was an honor almost more than he could comprehend. He was now holding her hand. Since they had been in the car, they had both been in a mostly passive mood. Both were afraid to express their true feelings. Both were disbelieving the good fortune of being together. But now, Robert was changing to active mood with help from above.

"Mary do you believe Jesus died for your sins and—"

She gleefully interrupted. "Yes! Yes! And Yes!"

Robert started crying and leaned toward Mary. Mary leaned. Clumsily, he cupped her heaving face in his shaking hands and started kissing her tear-soaked cheek before he found her trembling lips. While savoring the salt from her tears, Robert Arlington passed from the present to a dimension where angels receive and certify dreams. For years, he had been praying to find a Christian girl just like Mary.

The joy and pleasure of their first kiss would have to be labeled a double-header. It was a pledge of love and devotion, plus a kiss of rejoicing. Mary had just surrendered her heart to Jesus Christ, her Savior. Her saved heart almost exploded when she realized she was celebrating victory in Jesus with Robert.

They had to back away to gulp some much needed air. Neither knew how long the kiss lasted, but both knew they had wanted it to happen hours before. Robert was one foot from Mary when he opened his waterlogged eyes. His vision was blurred, and the light in the car was dim. But though it was ever so dim, he still saw the most beautiful, the most magnificent and the most glorious person ever. Her rosy cheeks, dripping with tears, glistened even in the small light. Her hair was half up and half down. From one foot away, her brown eyes looked black and shiny. At the instant his eyes focused, Mary was trying to smile while still crying tears of joy. The feeling that nothing else mattered they experienced earlier while holding hands was a walk around the block compared to the celestial trip presently in their hearts.

This angel before him was a pole apart from persona non grata. She was the "welcomest" person he had ever encountered. More welcome than even Pa Pa Lynn. With Mary, he could envision a life of . . . He checked his thoughts. His heart was racing faster than the sane part of his mind. His senses slowly returned to the present—one foot from Mary. Influenced by the magical force of cupid's love, they were drawn together again. The second kiss was also joy-filled and protracted, but a bit short of the explosion and resultant shock waves that rippled through their bodies and souls during the first kiss. When they came up for air, Robert told her to hold him tight because he might fly away.

Between first and second kisses, Robert had wondered if there might be a 'Celestial Bureau of Kisses' where angels observed and recorded the glory value of a kiss. If that were so, then the bar would need to be raised. He believed that first kiss was authorized by God Almighty the day they were born. And what's more, it just occurred to him that his co-worker's recommendation to visit the New England states must have also been directed by the Almighty.

They wisely utilized the next few minutes as a recovery period to harness some flyaway emotions—an interval when breathing would be regulated. A time to reflect on the long and eventful hours since their eyes and hearts first met. It was not a tumbling experience—just a soothing transition from unbelieving to accepting the trophy that God planned for them.

"You know Robert, I wish everyone could experience the joy of Jesus and the rapture of a first kiss at the same time—a destined first kiss."

"Robert, are you alright? Do you know you're crying?"

Robert Arlington, number 257826, was indeed crying. Both hands covered his face. Ralph turned off the tape recorder. It would be another few seconds before Robert looked at Ralph and smiled while shaking his head.

"I'm sorry. Those few minutes of my life made an indelible imprint on my heart. Thank you, Ralph. Before you pried me from my miry pool of depression, those precious moments were in a 'lock down' compartment of my mind."

Ralph Fenny walked out of the prison anticipating a first kiss with Michelle. With the way he felt right then, after hearing Robert's story, the bar was going to be raised again.

CHAPTER SIX

" . . . he met her at Tony's Place . . .

When Ralph stepped into the kitchen, his mother screamed from her bedroom, "Ralph! We have to go to Baltimore! Margaret fell—she's in intensive care. I'm already packed. We'll drive down tonight." Ralph closed his eyes and lowered his head.

In all his years, he had been a good son—never refusing his mother's requests. But tonight, he guessed history would be made. Instead of yielding to his mother's command, he was going to see Michelle. He was going to kiss her tonight—not when leaving, but when arriving. And of course, he would kiss her again when leaving—and some in between. For hours, he had wanted to see her tonight. He could hardly wait for her to hear Robert's tape.

Ralph was looking in the refrigerator when his mother rushed into the kitchen. "No Ralphy! We'll eat on the road. Margaret is really bad and may not live through the night."

As he closed the fridge door, Ralph thought, "Okay, I'll eat pizza with Michelle."

Fern Fenny was mostly an even-tempered person and had never pursued any great endeavor in life except being PTA president for five years. She had never wanted for anything and had never forced her will on anyone except her only child. Ralph looked at his mother with her short, red hair and flushed face. Her lips were about to disappear and her eyes were red from crying.

"Hurry and pack," she directed. "We'll be gone a few days— Oh, I don't know how long. She's bad, Ralphy."

He had never seen his mother so upset and he had never been in such a dilemma. Since meeting Michelle, mundane chapters in his life were pages behind him. He was now on a two-front crusade. He was charging with his center force of emotion and compassion to rescue Michelle from cruel hardships of life and give to her all the happiness he could extend. On his right flank, he was collecting evidence to free Robert from shackles of injustice. His confidence was mounting with Robert's case.

Still standing near the refrigerator, Ralph was determined to state his intentions for the evening. "Mother, I have plans . . . "

Interrupting as if not hearing her son's declaration, "Hurry and get packed—we must get started. Ben called two hours ago. It happened around noon in the bathroom. She hit her head on the tub." Fern was noticeably upset and gave this brief report in short spurts. Suddenly, more tears tumbled down her flushed cheeks. She ran to Ralph and put her arms around his neck. In between sobs, she pleaded, "Oh Ralphy! I don't want to lose my only sister."

Two hours later, a silver Lexus was going south on I-95 with a mother and son occupying the front seat. Neither had spoken for miles. Ralph had never much liked his Aunt Margaret and liked his Uncle Ben even less. His Uncle Ben had an aggressive personality with a loud mouth to go with it. He was a stevedore and told boisterous, dockside stories in which he was always the champion. Ralph was envisioning many hours with him while Mother would be by Aunt Margaret's bedside.

After leaving the prison, Ralph was riding on dreams never before conceived. He was scaling a mountain with the summit in sight until . . . He looked over toward his mother. She was asleep. In his dispirited heart, he realized her battle was won, and he was still charging—in the wrong direction. With his eyes back on the road, he thought about the definition of obedience.

He had stopped at Michelle's to see her and to leave Robert's last tape. She was gone, so he left a note. For the dismal miles ahead, he decided to think about his defense strategy for Robert.

Five miserable days and four long nights in Baltimore. Ralph had to admit that the Uncle Ben dread had been subjugated by Ben's unexpected concern for his wife. He spent hours at the hospital with his wife and sister-in-law. Ralph called Michelle to report his safe return and that his mother stayed in Baltimore—his Aunt was not expected to recover from her injuries. He also told Michelle that Mary was coming to the office tomorrow morning.

Their three phone conversations while he was in Baltimore were mostly about Robert's tape. Only two rental items were discussed. Nothing big—she and "Flash" made the problems go away. Ralph liked her descriptive use of words. What was missing in their conversations was the lack of reference to their last time together. In talking about Robert's tape, she did mention "Guardian Angel" one time but nothing about their tender moments together.

Ralph entered his office at nine to review the typed deposition. Michelle walked in at five to ten. She was wearing a dainty, floral print dress that snugly displayed her many curves. Ralph had never seen her this dressed-up before. She greeted him with a half smile as if to ask, "Do I look all right?" Ralph was still staring when she added cheerful words to her greeting.

"Good morning."

Initially, he only smiled and nodded while taking a deep draught of beauty she had been concealing from him. Her light blonde hair was pinned up in a way that seemed to crown the princess before him. Reluctantly, he retrieved his protruding eyes and happily returned her greeting.

"Good morning to you."

Mary walked in before any questions could be asked like, "Did you sleep well?" or "What do you think about this rain?"

When Mary Bly O'Day walked into any size room, heads would turn. She was tall and presented a regal vision for all who looked—and everyone would always feast on her grandeur. She was wearing a dark green jacket over a creamy blouse, with a complimentary plaid skirt. Her auburn hair glistened as it brushed her shoulders. Ralph was still inwardly rejoicing with the beauty of Michelle buzzing through his optic nerves—Mary almost overloaded them. As he was experiencing this double exposure of beauty, he thought, "What truly delightful examples of 'What God hath wrought.'"

After greetings and introductions, Ralph told Mary that Michelle was his real estate manager and his para-legal. Michelle glanced quickly at Ralph. Before any embarrassment about her second job, he told Mary she was typing the deposition and that was why she was present. He didn't want any gaps so he moved on, making a reference to their phone conversation. He told Mary again about the necessity of the deposition and again emphasized that he wasn't prying. He told her Robert had just finished about the restaurant parking lot conversation. A reminiscent shimmer edged her eyes that slowly advanced to a full-face glow.

"Yes, that was a great day for us." Mary had been sitting stiff and straight in her chair since arriving, and this was her first real smile since forcing a couple during introductions. Ralph knew from their phone conversation that she was reluctant to talk about her private relationship with Robert. He was purposely being slow getting started.

Looking at Mary, Michelle spoke for the first time since the intros. "Tea or coffee?"

If Michelle could have read Ralph's mind, she would have agreed with Robert that Mary was beautiful, and her presence in a room did indeed command attention. Michelle had on her best dress today. She had thoughts that Mary might be looking for someone like Ralph. Michelle liked him and didn't want to be perceived as a poor girl (wearing a Goodwill dress) looking for a meal ticket. Nevertheless, she was going to fight for Ralph the best way she could. If she only knew how he had dreamed and yearned to kiss her, she could have worn jeans today.

Conversation during the morning tea party was unhurried. Michelle had made some small, cake donuts, garnished with brown sugar and cinnamon; they were well received. After a short period when Ralph talked about his Aunt Margaret and his Baltimore trip, he placed the recorder on the desk. As a preamble, he started with the date and stated that it was still raining at ten twenty-five.

Mary knew she was the center of attraction as she stared at the recorder. Ralph and Michelle were focused on her when they saw an imperceptible change on her pretty face. She seemed to shift from the present into a short-interval time warp as she softly spoke.

"We left the restaurant parking lot and went to my house. It wasn't late but our day had been so intense and spiritual that we needed to get our feet back to earth. I doubt if you can understand how glorified and elevated I felt that night. I had the love of Jesus in my heart and a tall, handsome angel crowded in there too. The Lord must have sent Robert to me."

She appeared to recirculate the events of that unforgettable day as she continued. "I doubt you can understand how I felt." Ralph glanced at Michelle who seemed to be in her own time warp. Mary looked over her audience's heads as if collecting thoughts she had long ago flung asunder—memories that had become excess baggage since Robert was gone forever. Thus far, she had not shown any expectation that Robert's status would change. She agreed to talk about their relationship, not knowing Ralph's ability or dedication regarding Robert's freedom. And she certainly didn't have any reason to realize how much Michelle would contribute. She had painfully testified at the trial and would again. Right now, she would continue telling them about falling in love with Robert. She was now willing to talk about the happiest time in her life even though they were no longer engaged.

"Mother! I have been to Heaven." Skipping around the room, Mary told in a singsong gibber that she and an angel sat on Heaven's doorstep and then slowly descended back to earth locked in each other's arms. Maureen looked at her daughter's blissful face, but disappointment showed on her own face. She had failed to prevent her daughter from going out with that stranger from West Virginia. Mary didn't play with her mother's emotions too long before proudly telling her all about that hillbilly rascal from West Virginia.

After Mary was in bed and had retrieved the pieces of her exploded heart, she decided to invite Robert to a Saturday brunch. The menu flew together while she dialed the motel number. A few minutes later, she put down the phone.

Robert had checked out of his room thirty minutes earlier. The desk clerk had just reported for duty and didn't know the checkout reason nor that Robert had been reassigned to another room. For nearly an hour, Mary relived every minute and every feeling of the day and evening. Then suddenly, she was consumed with pain so intense she became woozy from not breathing. She remembered some previously overlooked words—"to hold him tight because he might fly away."

In a reluctant comprehension of understanding, she whispered, "That must be it! He is an angel or *was* an angel, and now he's gone back to Heaven." She cried for hours—pleading to understand why this should happen to her. She repeatedly asked God how this could happen. What in her life had she done to deserve this? She cried until there were no more tears. She was sleeping at 9:00 a.m. when her mother gently woke her.

"Mary, Robert called." Maureen was expecting her "daughter-in-love" to jump from the bed eager to talk with him. Maureen repeated that Robert had called. After a few turns in bed, Mary asked with all the sarcasm her personality would permit. "Did you say he called or did he send an air-mail letter from Heaven?"

"What are you saying child?"

"Mother! I'm saying he checked out—he's not on this earth anymore."

Confused with such a statement, Maureen demanded an explanation. "Mary! What do you mean? I just talked with Robert Arlington. You know, that nice man from West Virginia. He's in the hospital."

That bit of earthly news quickly prompted Mary to sit up in bed. "What! What did he say Mother? Is he okay? What happened?"

"Now Mary, calm down, and I'll tell you what he said. He went to his motel room last night after leaving here, and his room was flooded from a broken water pipe."

Maureen knew to hurry—Mary was wide-eyed with her mouth opened. "He was assigned another room. After that, he was walking on the parking lot and walked in front of a car." Mary tried to move her lips. "He's okay with cuts and bruises and a suspected mild concussion—the car was moving slowly."

Mary jumped out of bed.

"I'm going to see him."

"No dear, he's getting released around noon."

Mary settled down and told her mother about calling the motel last night and about her conclusion that he was an angel who had returned to Heaven.

Robert arrived at the O'Day house a few minutes before five. Mary had talked with him at the hospital, and instead of brunch, they would have dinner at six. Robert was impressed with the presentation, taste, and texture of the feast.

"Oh this is so heavenly—better than food at home."

Mary's words were mingled with a tittering, "See Mother, we have an angel in our midst."

The meal was truly a success with conversation and laughter unhurriedly served in abundance. Robert told about walking

in front of the car because he was looking up, trying to con-
nect the stars to form an outline of the angel he had just met.
Mary interjected, "Here in Vermont, we stop and give cars
right-of-way."

This started another round of car and pedestrian jokes.
Maureen didn't say it, but Mary sensed that her mother was
beginning to like this stranger from down south. The two young
ones were finally ordered to the back porch. Without protest,
they walked out the kitchen door laughing. Once seated on
the glider with large decorator pillows on both ends, Robert
thanked Mary for the excellent meal. The kiss that followed
was mutually desired and enjoyed.

After their hearts descended, his dreamy eyes focused on
the backyard landscaping. Minutes before, he couldn't have
recounted the many shrubs and flowers that Maureen had lovingly planted and groomed. He had been mostly thinking about
his next move, which was no move at all. So now as he gazed
at the beautiful backyard, he knew his New England vacation
had changed to whatever Vermont could offer with Mary by
his side. Through their clasped hands, he could feel the same
sentiments passing from her heart to his.

After this short period of adjusting to their newfound direction, Robert slowly spoke. "You know Mary, I wouldn't be
sitting beside you now if it hadn't been for a recommendation
by my best friend. Did I tell you about Mason who also works
at the power company?"

Mary displayed a little lip curl as if trying to remember.

"Well anyway, I just thought about it. Mason suggested
I take a vacation in the New England states. We've been together since grade school—played football in high school. We
have hunted and fished together for many years. He's a line
maintenance supervisor while I'm with engineering, but we
work together occasionally."

Robert stopped talking and glanced at Mary who had a pleasant contentment shining on her pretty face.

"Now Mary dear, don't laugh when I tell you Mason's last name. It's Dixon—Mason Dixon."

Mary didn't laugh. She just looked at him with a strange glare. Then suddenly, she exploded—words and laughter were mingled together. "Of course! I remember some geography. That's some of West Virginia's northern boundary with Pennsylvania. But, why would parents name a baby that?"

"Well, I'll tell my favorite person from Vermont. His mother's brother was named Mason. Guess they didn't think how it sounded together. But it doesn't matter. Mr. Mason Dixon is the reason I'm right now sitting beside the most beautiful, the most—"

Mary put her hand over his mouth, which led to a soul-stirring kiss. A few heartbeats later, they sensed a dangerous curve ahead. Reluctantly, they braked their speeding emotions and stared at the backyard landscaping. Before the tingle had subsided, Robert almost cooed as he proclaimed, "You know Mary, I'm not sure I could be happier."

"I feel it too."

Robert was content and relaxed and thankful that Mason pointed him north. His favorite vacation place had been Myrtle Beach, South Carolina. That's where he and Mason did their freedom thing after high school graduation. Suddenly, springing from deep thought, he pondered aloud.

"I wonder why he recommended up here?"

"Who?" Mary, too, had been in deep thought.

"Mason."

"Oh yes."

Robert smiled as he continued. "He has never been north of the Mason-Dixon Line."

Mary also smiled as the pun was acknowledged. Then Robert asked in a pensive tone. "Would you like to hear a story

about Mason that will explain the sort of man I have for my best friend?"

"Sure. I would like to know more about your friends."

"Okay. Mason and I went fishing this past May. We fish often, but this night was a little different. We backpacked to the stream and stayed overnight—like we always did. Sometimes we would go alone when the other one was busy, but this warm Friday night we were together. Mason had been a bit moody the whole evening. We had settled down to sleep under the stars when he asked if I knew how he met Mary Ellen. I told him I guessed at church since that's where I saw them together for the first time.

Robert looked at Mary for a long second.

"Some people won't believe this true story."

"I will." After a short pause, "Robert, I've only known you for a few hours, but truly believe you to be the most good and honest person I've ever met." During this little parley, Mary maintained eye contact with her earth angel. Robert was happily encouraged to continue.

"Before I go on, let me say that I believe God is controlling our lives—I mean controlling everyone."

Mary squeezed his hand while agreeing.

"Yes, I now know some of God's ways."

"I've thought a lot about this since last May. He didn't meet her at church—he met her at Tony's Place on a Thursday night before they came to church the following Sunday. It was August a year ago. Mason knew Mary Ellen in High School as a girl with a "reputation", but didn't know what happened to her until almost a year ago. She was a year behind him and was known as Ellen Cyrus. He had never dated her."

It was almost 10:00 p.m. when Mason entered Tony's Place. Ellen was sitting on a barstool with her eyes fixed on her drink. He walked straight to her. His voice rippled with embarrassment.

"Ellen . . . I would like for us to go camping and fishing tomorrow night."

She looked up at the handsome man through bleary eyes. Before she had a chance to answer, Mason continued what he had been practicing to say.

"You don't need to take anything except a jacket and sturdy shoes."

Her mind was already numbed from more than a few drinks, and this "dumbo" was muttering about a jacket and sturdy shoes.

"What are you talking about mister?"

"Ellen, my name is Mason Dixon . . . we . . . we were in high school together . . . I played football."

She had not thought about those unhappy years for what seemed like a century. The many hours spent on her barstool in this smoke-filled room had caused her to think of only one night at a time and the next drink. She concluded long ago when happiness changes to misery, memories can be a curse. Ellen Cyrus was a prostitute in Tony's Place—Mason knew this. She decided to take a good look at this weirdo before contributing one of her better high school attributes to the conversation.

"I was a cheerleader."

"I know. You were the best one. I was just a year ahead of you—I played football. I would often admire your enthusiasm and your skill." Ellen would probably never be a beauty queen, but she was definitely pretty. Later, when she would get off her barstool, Mason would note that she still had her trim high school figure.

She suspiciously looked at him trying to discern his motive. She knew a lot about men's motives.

"Listen Mr. Football Player, you'll have to check into a room if you want to talk to me."

Tony's Place was locally referred to as a "beer joint." The bar room was once a grand dining room of a rather grand three-story hotel. Now Tony's Place was, at best, a sleazy place. Ten rooms on the second floor were for rent—one was rented several times the same night.

This was Mason's first time in Tony's. He followed instructions, and five minutes later after he paid fifty dollars, Ellen walked into his room. She started to slowly remove her sweater. Mason threw up his hand and spoke in a calm voice.

"Leave it on and sit on the bed beside me."

Apparently that didn't seem too weird, so she sat down. In the few minutes since they first met, Mason detected that some of her callus seemed to have softened. He again mentioned the camping in a more positive delivery than before.

"Like I said, you don't have to take anything except a jacket and good hiking shoes or boots. I will have all the food and equipment and fishing tackle. I have done this many times with my friend Robert, but this time I want you to go with me. We drive for about one hour and then backpack for thirty minutes or so. I will carry most everything—all the heavy stuff. I know you'll like it Ellen."

Mason paused before continuing. "It is so peaceful by the river with a campfire."

Ellen was listening but not looking at Mason. She had already been in this room two times tonight and now number three was talking about something peaceful. That frame of mind had long ago been replaced with recurring avalanches of turbulence that were keeping her thoughts in a blur of shame and guilt.

When he stopped to breathe, Ellen seemed sullen and distrustful when she asked, "Why are you doing this? Why are you here tonight?"

He tightened his lips and looked at her profile. When she turned to him, he barely uttered, "I don't know. I just feel that this is something good. Something that . . . well . . . I just want to be with you."

Last night or earlier tonight, had a man said that to her, she would have replied, "So you want to be with me, well stupid I'm here. Let's get on with it." But tonight, it was all different. Maybe that word "peaceful" was stirring a feeling reminiscent of a better time in her life when she had known a bit of decency. During her high school years, and before, she had so wanted to belong and have friends that she traded her body for what she thought was friendship. During those unhappy years, she became an alcoholic. So after high school, Tony provided her booze and she was paid for doing what she used to do for free.

Mason suddenly stood up and told her to meet him at the bus station tomorrow afternoon at five. As he left the room, he told her that everything would be provided and they would have a pleasant, relaxing time together.

Ellen wasn't used to positive statements about guiltless things in life.

Robert was repeating Mason's instructions about meeting at the bus station when Maureen beckoned them into the kitchen. She announced that Mary had a surprise for Robert. Once in the kitchen, Mary disappeared but promptly returned proudly carrying a beautiful coconut creme pie.

Mary looked at her watch. She suddenly reverted to the nervous, tense person that had arrived two hours ago. She didn't say anything about another appointment, but was obviously anxious to leave. Mary glanced up at Ralph with begging eyes.

"I'm sorry, I must go."

"Can you return tomorrow?"

"Yes, but could we start at nine?

Ralph assured her that would be fine.

After two hours of talking about Robert and Mason, she was suddenly gone. Michelle and Ralph sat for a long time filled with empathy for Mary.

CHAPTER SEVEN

"Mary, I love you."

"I'm sorry for calling so late Mary. My Aunt who lives in Baltimore just died. I'll call later and reschedule our next meeting."

"That's okay Mr. Fenny. Just let me know."

Ralph then called Michelle. She had just finished typing Mary's part of the deposition and announced to Ralph that she thought Mary was hiding something. Michelle philosophically talked some without directly revealing her prediction. Ralph tried to persuade her to tell him what she thought. She would only say, "Later."

Ralph almost pointedly asked if he could come over and kiss her goodbye. While contemplating this bold thought, there was a lull in their conversation. Michelle broke the silence.

"Ralph?"

"Oh . . . yes I'm here." There was another brief period of nothing on the phone line. Then he heard her sweet voice again that seemed to be wrapped in layers of concern.

"Ralph . . . be careful and hurry back. I will . . . I'll be . . . How many days 'til you're back?"

"Shouldn't be many. Mother may want to . . . No! It will be just a few days. I'll see to it."

Ralph stared in the direction of the phone for a long time after their goodbye. Their short conversation was strained—he couldn't say what was in his heart and apparently she couldn't either. Before he went to bed, he had definitely decided to tell Mother about Michelle. He would tell her exactly how he was feeling toward her and that he was going to marry her. Whee! What faith—since he had never even kissed her. He decided to tell his mother after the funeral, on the way back home.

Ralph stayed awake for two hours honestly expecting Michelle to call and invite him over for a cup of tea and a kiss.

Ralph was in Baltimore only four days, and to Michelle's surprise, Fern Fenny did not return with him. She was staying to help Ben with post-funeral affairs. Ralph explained to Michelle that his uncle was a changed person, especially in the presence of his mom. He was more soft-spoken and more courteous. His mother had also changed—she laughed more and seemed to enjoy garnering the attention and compliments he so freely scattered her way. Ralph first noticed this change when they were together at the hospital while his Aunt Margaret was in ICU. He believed his mother was nearing a major turn in her life and also believed she would soon live with her new husband in Baltimore. It might become really easy to announce his intentions toward Michelle. He wanted to say "his engagement," but of course he couldn't say that yet.

Three days later, Ralph was back at the prison. Mary cancelled their second meeting. He didn't ask why, and she didn't volunteer a reason. When told of this, Robert didn't respond. Ralph brought him up to date with what Mary had talked about.

Sunday was another interesting day for Robert and Mary. They went to church and then had lunch with her Aunt Molly who lived "way out" (ten miles from Montpelier) according to Molly. The food was good and they enjoyed lunch with Maureen's only sister Molly Kathleen McClanahan, who had never been married. Maureen recently remarked to Mary that she believed her forty-six year old sister would never get married—she had her cats and rocking chair and seemed to be totally content.

After lunch, the two young friends walked up a hill out back of the house. The sun was warm, and a cool breeze was trying to frizzle Mary's hair until she tied it into a ponytail. The view was spectacular even from Robert's reference to the hills and valleys of his beloved West Virginia. From their vantage point, they could see for miles. The sky was a dreamy azure expanse with foamy white clouds lazily drifting to another state. They could see a checker-board array of mowed hay fields, pasture land, and a hundred shades of color from brown to blue to green and to red and yellow apples on thousands of trees aligned in rows like soldiers standing at attention. Interspersed were painted barns with nearby cows munching on tender blades of rain nourished grass.

Arteries of transportation crisscrossed the picture in a most interesting pattern. Some were parallel, some crossed like a plus sign, some were T's and some were skewed from the others as if their origin started from animal paths. Lush trees outlined streams, making them prominent as they meandered from farm to farm. Riding on the cool breeze was a mixture of newly mown hay and a dozen other scents indigenous of a Vermont summer afternoon. The two young friends, who met only a couple of days earlier, were ten feet apart as they silently viewed this panoramic gift from God. Robert turned and looked at Mary as her beauty flanked nature's pictorial contribution to his moistened eyes. He suddenly knew it was the right time to say what was burning in his heart.

"Mary, I love you."

Mary Bly O'Day turned her head in Robert's direction. She didn't say anything, and she didn't move. She could only think, "What a lovely Sunday afternoon." It was two seconds and three strides later, when she tackled Robert with her arms around his neck—they both hit the ground. Before he could catch his breath, she replied to his declaration.

"You big hillbilly, I have loved you from the time I saw you standing in the doorway."

The kiss that followed may have exceeded the glory of their first kiss. This kiss was backed up with the full knowledge that they had surrendered all inhibitions. No more restraints regarding action, emotions, or thoughts. When the two happy, contented souls unlocked their arms and rolled to their backs, Robert looked at his wristwatch. He quickly calculated their time together.

"It has been fifty-two hours and a few ticks since we met. Can you believe it?" Not giving Mary time to answer, "Why didn't I say 'I love you' the minute my eyes first saw you?"

"Are all West Virginians that slow? Really—fifty-two hours to say what was in your heart."

Robert was too content to even move his lips. He was watching clouds change their shape as they slowly moved south. Mary must have been doing the same, for she didn't say anything for minutes. But her mind and heart were conferring about a secret dream that had been nourished by many seasons of warm afternoons. In soft, hushed words, results of her thoughts were announced.

"I have been coming up to this spot for many years, mostly on Sunday afternoons. I would lie on my back, just like now, and watch the clouds and dream. My dreams would be about someone like you. My mind would often drift from real time consciousness to a dimension of ineffable beauty—a place too sacred and wonderful to tread. I would float along a glittering rainbow and find my dream man at the end with outstretched arms. We would embrace and whisper about future plans. I started sliding down that dreamy rainbow fifty-two hours ago."

Robert quickly glanced at his watch. "How 'bout fifty-two hours and twelve minutes?"

The stimulus for any more poetic thoughts or words had been crushed with his correction. "Ohhh! Are all engineers that precise?"

"Well, the good ones are to insure safety of life and limb."

"Let me tell you something, Mr. Engineer, I love you and your accurate arithmetic. I can't imagine anything or anyone coming between us."

Just after 'anyone coming between us' was transmitted from her dry mouth, she realized those four words sounded like a proposal. She immediately wanted to retract or explain, but she did neither. The words were from her heart and would be recorded unabridged.

In this idyllic setting, these two young, earthly beings, so much committed to each other, could not know how the 'spring of life' would soon unwind for them. A coming event,

incomprehensible to both, would test every ounce of their faith in each other and faith in their Heavenly Father. No degree of insight or keenness of mind could prepare them to cope with gathering storm clouds on their seemingly bright horizon. When the spring broke, the backlash of the twang would create a chasm between their hearts painfully converse to the closeness at that moment.

Mary had rolled partially onto Robert with her heart pressed directly on his. This scene would be remembered during many lonely times—lonely and forlorn hours when the only incentive to reach for another tomorrow was their belief in Jesus and the blessed hope of an eternity with Him.

CHAPTER EIGHT

. . . she slept uninterrupted . . .

At ten o'clock Monday morning, Robert was putting a large picnic basket into the car. Today's itinerary was to relax and to sightsee and to enjoy some of Vermont's treasures. Yesterday they ascended to a new plateau. From their higher plane of commitment, they were eager to herald to the world that they were in love. And if anyone couldn't see it, they were ready to volunteer the happy news.

Robert was impressed with the picnic lunch that included three different kinds of sandwiches, crackers, and spreads. All were seasoned with easy conversation and sprinkled with several dashes of gaiety. After accolades were heaped on the chef for a lovely luncheon, they moved from the picnic table to a grassy knoll overlooking a small lake. Once seated on the blanket, both were absorbed with the placid view. Neither wanted to be moved from their peaceful reverie. The short morning had been crowded with happy times, including a maple syrup exhibition complete with a small cone of maple flavored ice cream. They were indeed happy and content to be close and to feel the magnetism of love pulling on their heart strings.

After some silent mellow time, Mary asked Robert without looking at him, "What happened with Mason and Ellen?"

"Ah yes!"

"I've been thinking about them. Did she go camping with him?"

In the quietness of this Vermont summer afternoon, Robert was looking at the glassy, still lake darkened with shadows of southbound clouds. He was remembering about Mason and Ellen. Suddenly, he was encompassed within an essence of quintessential delight as his thoughts focused on Jesus—the most perfect manifestation of God's love. He closed his eyes, and rejoiced in the fact that Jesus forgives ALL sins. He also knew that the Lord could bring two people together. He saw it with Mason and Ellen, and then he was directed to Mary.

"Yes, she went with him on the camping, slash fishing trip."

Mason arrived at the Bus Station at fifteen 'til five. He was packed and ready for his camping partner to appear. At five 'til, a stray doubt fluttered by as he sat in his truck. After their brief meeting last night, he had confidently planned and packed for Ellen to accompany him. At five o'clock, an avalanche of doubts flew by his closed eyes. Then—the sight and sound of a cavalry unit arriving in the nick of time couldn't have been more glorious than the sight of Ellen silently stepping outside the terminal door. Mason was standing beside his pickup truck when their eyes met. He walked to her and took the small bag from her left hand.

"Hi Ellen, I see you're left-handed, too."

"Yep, been that way since I was a pup."

Both smiled.

On the drive to where he would park the truck, neither talked much. Mason made a comment about the warm weather and also mentioned that it had been a month since his last fishing trip. He asked if she had fished much.

She answered, "Only a little."

Important about their scant conversation were the words that were not spoken. He didn't shower her with praise for being at the bus station. He didn't further try to persuade her that she would enjoy camping. Mason didn't know at the time that Ellen had already started to change. After he left the hotel last night, she went to her room instead of back on her barstool. She had some latitude with her duty time except on weekends. She drank no more last night and none today. For the first time in years, she slept uninterrupted with no morning hangover and no morning guilt. It seemed to her that the appearance of Mason last night eradicated the guilt from the two previous trips to her business room.

Backpacking to the campsite was more invigorating than strenuous. The only talking was when Mason would say something about a tree or a vine or an animal. When at the campsite, he had a blazing fire in a few minutes, and Ellen was to mind the fire while he caught fish for supper. The four bass he caught were cleaned and ready to cook forty minutes later. He put each fish in aluminum foil. Into the inside of each fish he poured a mixture of melted butter and the herbs, rosemary and oregano, plus salt and black pepper. He then squeezed juice from a lemon to complete the seasoning. While they were slowly cooking in hot coals, he warmed pre-cooked baby carrots and fried a few strips of bacon.

The frying bacon permeated the warm air connecting Ellen with a pristine time in her past. When she was a young child, her favorite Aunt and Uncle would take her and her first cousins camping. The aroma of the frying bacon triggered a period in her life before . . . she couldn't finish the thought. In the same skillet with the bacon, Mason sliced pre-peeled potatoes and in another skillet, he fried a hushpuppy mix—flat like small pancakes. During the meal, Ellen was still marveling at Mason's skill and speed in preparing the delicious food. Since she had never cooked much, she was really impressed by him.

Ellen didn't feel threatened with Mason. She was cautious, however, while sorting through recent memories and thoughts trying to find out why she was here with this good-looking man who had just served her a gourmet meal. She had heard somewhere on her way down to the gutter that there were no free meals. She had been in many scary situations, but tonight was not a bit scary—except she was afraid all this wasn't real.

After Mason cleaned up the campfire area, they both went fishing. Ellen caught three and laughed and laughed and screamed when she fell in the river while bringing in the big one. Mason always had some dry clothes for emergencies. The novice angler started to feel like a real person as they conversed after catching the fish. She was soon acting like a seasoned camper (in his much too big for her walking shorts and pocket tee) as she gathered firewood. She had brought a change of underclothes. Instead of drying them with her jeans and shirt, she put the wet lingerie in her bag.

Later, after a short hike, Mason placed a blanket and a sleeping bag on each side of the fire. Ellen reclined and slowly absorbed the majestic beauty of the stars. She had never been this close to tranquility. A calmness was creeping over her inner being. Ever since falling in the river, she felt cleaner. She knew that didn't wash away her sins, but somehow, it seemed that soil from her past was dissolving. One bit of her past, however, was immediately troubling her. A year ago, she went camping with two men. They rented her and took turns with her during the night. In the sober peacefulness of this night, guilt from that session was suddenly greater than the times at Tony's.

Mason propped up his head on his backpack and started playing his harmonica. The lonesome sound of the harmonica twisted through the glow of the campfire and wistfully transported her heart back to a chaste time in her life. She repeatedly drifted from the present to a young Ellen as he played familiar songs like "Red River Valley," "Home on the Range," and several of Stephen Foster's songs. By her request, he played "Blue Eyes Crying in the Rain." She couldn't stop the tears when he played "When My Blue Moon Turns to Gold Again."

Before some abusive things happened to her, she had attended church and had sung in the youth choir. Right now, she couldn't remember if she had so much as hummed since then. When "What a Friend We Have in Jesus" was played, she actually sang a few words. Mason played for another thirty minutes and the changing Ellen sang some more.

When the harmonica was cased, muted night sounds blended with rippling water rushing over stones in the stream. While nature's symphony was filling her ears, her happy eyes were feasting on the sky where a crescent moon looked ready to set sail across the diamond-studded vastness. It seemed to Ellen that some kind of magic was circling about the campsite, weaving a shroud of serenity over them. Over two young people—one afraid to surrender her true feelings and accept the will of God knocking on her heart. She was afraid to believe that the happiness enrapturing her whole being was real. And she didn't know that her many sins could disappear in an instant like the flittering campfire sparks melting into the warm night air. Ellen quietly cried for a long, long time before peacefully drifting to sleep.

"Well, there you have it. Ellen and Mason slept under the stars." When Robert looked at Mary, she was crying.

"Oh Robert, that was so beautiful. All of it—the frying bacon, the harmonica and singing, the night sounds and rippling water and the stars and moon. I bet Ellen will never forget that night, including falling in the river and actually having clean fun. Do you know why Mason went to Tony's Place?"

"No, and he doesn't know either, unless it was Ellen's guardian angel who directed him."

Mary hesitated and then softly spoke. "I can also believe that."

Before another word, large raindrops suddenly broke up their quiet time on the grassy knoll. While Robert was telling about Mason and Ellen, the storyteller and Mary didn't notice that clouds sailing down from Canada had become darker and lower. It seemed the treetops ripped out their bottoms, dumping tons of rain to the ground. The tour guide and her charge were fairly soaked before getting into the car.

After a few reflective miles on road, Mary asked what he wanted to do tomorrow.

"I want to be with you."

"Okay, but where do *you* want to go?"

She emphasized "you."

"Wherever you go . . . "

"Robert! What did that rain do to you?"

"It soaked into my brain and short-circuited some cells. I now only want to be near you."

"Okay! You can be near me tomorrow at Burlington and Lake Champlain."

There was another silent time until Robert asked, "How about dinner tonight at a—"

Mary interrupted. "Only if we go to the Chef's Table on Main Street."

"Agreed, my love."

After only a relatively few hours together, two young people, with as many differences as similarities, were conversing without inhibitions. An invisible thread of Herculean strength tied them together. A thread that would later stretch to dangerous limits but would prevail against determined forces.

By the time they arrived at Mary's house, they also agreed to take a short nap in their respective bedrooms. When Robert reclined on his bed at the motel, the rain had changed to a gentle summer shower. The soothing, rhythmic sound of the steady, soft rain lulled him to a peaceful sleep.

Robert was to be at Mary's around six-thirty He awoke at seven-thirty. When Mary answered the phone, he asked, "The dinner date tonight—was that eastern or central time?" Not giving her a chance to answer, he continued. "Mary, I'm sorry—I just woke and—"

"Robert! Do you know what 'ditto' means?"

"Yes."

"Well, I just woke from a dreamy nap. You rescued me from Andy Blake. Andy and I were in grade school together and he used to chase me all the time."

"Oh boy! Was I on a white horse?"

"I think so."

Maureen had eaten alone, and with her leftovers as a base, they decided to eat at Mary's house.

They again sat on the back porch glider after another great meal. Mary knew how to garnish to please both sight and taste. Following a brief period of relaxing their minds and bodies, Mary asked where Mason and Ellen were now.

"Ah, they are happily married and living a few doors from his mother. Did I say they were married last Christmas?"

Mary moved her head in a negative way.

"Well, they were after meeting in August. Let's go back to the camping trip for a minute."

Mason had breakfast ready when Ellen opened her contented eyes. They hiked after that until lunchtime, when he prepared a nice picnic lunch that included canned, boned chicken. The morning was a bonding time even though conversation was mostly about flora and fauna. Mason was a true outdoorsman, possessing a vast knowledge of nature. On the way back to town, Ellen changed from a carefree, laughing girl to a solemn girl void of speech or happy expression. During this new day in her life, she had jabbered and marveled about so many earthly treasures she had previously overlooked. She was sitting next to the truck door mute and still. Just before arriving at the city limits, she blurted, "I'm not going back to that place!"

Mason pulled the truck over onto the berm. After a few minutes, it was decided she would sleep at his mother's house. He went to Tony's and got a few of her things. Most of her personal items were left in the room. A young, changed girl, and a new friend who she thought might be an angel, went shopping for some new clothes after respectfully being accepted into the Dixon home.

Two weeks later, Ellen was saved from hell when she accepted Jesus as her personal savior. That's when her sins, ALL of them, were washed away. The love of Jesus filled her heart, causing her to know, by simple faith, that by believing He died for ALL her sins—she was forgiven.

"That's all about the camping trip. The full name of this new Christian had always been Mary Ellen. Before her guardian angel tapped Mason on his shoulder, she didn't feel worthy to use the Mary part. After Jesus changed her life, she's now proud to have the same name as His mother."

Mary Bly O'Day knew there was at least one more chapter to this story. But for now, the storyteller needed a kiss. Through this kiss, she wanted to transmit her thankfulness to him for asking if she wanted to be a Christian.

CHAPTER NINE

She could feel a flush on her face.

When Robert and Mary had come down from the hill out back of Aunt Molly's house yesterday afternoon, a girl was on the back porch waiting for them. She rose from the porch swing and greeted them—rather loudly. Tracy Evans was one of Mary's high school friends. She had maintained contact with her through the years mainly because she lived next to Aunt Molly. Tracy was not a close friend, but Mary cordially introduced Robert as an old friend from West Virginia.

"Well, Mary dear, where have you been hiding your handsome West Virginian? We have known each other for years, and this is the first time I've seen him."

Tracy was obviously attracted to Robert—but she was attracted to most males. She was not beautiful, but did have some rather superlative assets as revealed by her tight tee shirt and jeans. Long, straight, brown hair framed her semi-oval face. Her entrancing, black eyes had charmed many men who had ventured close to her wispy body. Looking only at Robert, she invited them to a chuck wagon party Saturday night. Before either could say that Robert was leaving on Thursday, she started with some details. She made it clear she expected to dance with him and also quickly told him there would be a lot more to do than just dance and eat.

For the first few miles, Mary was remembering the short scene with Tracy. Robert was also quiet this Tuesday morning on the way to Burlington. She was thinking, "Tracy might be thin and petite, but her aggressive personality seems to make her big and overpowering enough to take what ever she wants." Mary was particularly remembering what she had said about "a lot more" to do at the party.

"Robert, a penny for your thoughts."

He hesitated before answering, "I was . . . I was thinking about . . . about lunch. Have you been to Burlington before?"

"Yes—double dated with Tracy."

He quickly looked at Mary with disbelief. He knew she and Tracy were not kindred friends or likely candidates to double date. Before Robert questioned her, she interjected a comment into his thoughts.

"Just kidding."

Robert didn't say anything. Mary knew for sure that he was thinking about Tracy. She decided to change the subject.

"Robert?"

He glanced at her.

"Did you say Mason and Mary Ellen were doing okay now?"

"Oh yes, but last April she did encounter a situation at

church. She was summoned to a deacon's meeting—I think it was a Monday. Yes, it was Monday. Let me think a minute. He drove for another mile before he spoke again.

"There! Up there, I'll pull over and tell you what Mason said about that meeting with the deacons. He told me on our fishing trip last May."

After the Sunday night service, Tom Hicks told Mason that the deacons wanted to meet with Mary Ellen. Mason questioned the reason for the meeting. Mr. Hicks, senior deacon, would only reply that a situation came before the deacon board, and that Mary Ellen might help solve the problem. Since Mason's nature was to always help in any way he could, he encouraged his wife to help the deacons. Mason Dixon was a grand person but not without a rather innocent fault. He trusted everyone and seemed to see only the good side of people. Mary Ellen had spent most of life seeing and experiencing the bad side of her earthly male co-inhabitants and knew the kind of help the deacons wanted from her. Even having been around many honorable men in the church, she was still generally skeptical of men's motives.

Soon after starting to church with Mason, she and Sissy Carter became good friends. A lot of the church members were friendly, which she thought might have been due to their respect for Mason. But Sissy was different. She embraced her as an individual. She was Mary Ellen—not Mason's wife.

They would shop together and sometimes have lunch while resting before another sprint through the mall. After two months together, Sissy's personality became clear as being a lot like Mason. Her virtuous and wholesome heart didn't have room for weighing and considering a person's true intent. She seemed only to see the surface. Consequently, she did not see the wolf under her husband's fleecy façade. Mary Ellen had not seen Sissy's husband, Ollie, at Church until two Sundays ago.

She knew he recognized her when he maneuvered through the crowd after church to get close enough to say, "Nice to see you again." She saw him again the following Thursday. She was to meet Sissy at her house before going to the mall. When she arrived, Ollie answered the door saying Sissy would be ready soon. She stepped into the living room to wait and soon realized Sissy was on an unexpected errand. Ollie walked toward her with glassy eyes and whispered, "Ellen, I've missed you at Tony's." Without taking a breath, he propositioned her, "Sissy won't be back for thirty minutes. We could—"

Mary Ellen might have set a speed record when she flew out of the house. Later, without explanation, she apologized to Sissy for not keeping their appointment. Oh yes, she knew what kind of help the deacons wanted from her. The remaining part of that Sunday, the meeting was on her mind, but she was not really upset. When this young Christian went to bed, she prayed and asked the Lord to help her get through the meeting. She again thanked Jesus for making her a new, clean person and again thanked Him for his continuous love. As she was thanking Jesus for Mason, a glorious relaxing feeling flooded her inner being. Peaceful sleep stilled her vocal chords as she whispered, "Thank you Jesus—thank you Jesus—thank you . . . "

The next morning was mostly a typical Monday morn. Mason went to work, and Mary Ellen busied herself around the house until time to get ready. She was a little apprehensive while getting herself presentable for her day in court. The new girl that Jesus saved from guilt and shame didn't use much makeup now. Getting ready this Monday was pretty much routine, except a for little extra time spent with her hair—she didn't pin it up often.

When she walked into the Sunday school classroom, five judicial looking men were sitting on the front row, shoulder to shoulder. A lone chair had been placed in the front of the room. Mary Ellen looked squarely at her judges and delivered a cheerful "Good morning" while walking straight to her chair. Not giving them a chance to speak, she began speaking softly.

"Gentlemen, I want to tell you a story about a young girl who used to sing in a church choir. She lived with her grandmother because her parents were killed in a small plane crash. She sensed early that her grandmother really didn't want to raise her and extended only rationed love and care. To feel like a family member, she innocently turned to a first cousin for attention. He didn't waste much time before raping her. While he repeatedly took advantage of her, he warned her not to tell. He then taught her to drink beer that she soon learned to like. This young girl matured and was popular in high school for all the wrong reasons."

Mary Ellen was talking fast. Whatever they were going to say to her had to wait. She wanted to first tell what was in her heart. Tom Hicks, a trim and tan small man, was seated to her left. Next to him was a jolly-looking man in his thirties. His face was round with rosy cheeks that were resting on a plump double chin. His receding reddish hair was combed straight back. The next man was about as thin and wiry as Tom Hicks but much taller. His boney knees were well forward of the other knees lined up on the front row. Black curly hair covered half of his brow with the other half nearly covered by a strip of continuous eyebrows. The only one she had talked to was the next man, Jerry, who sang in the choir. He was overweight, completely bald, and in his fifties. The last of the solemn deacons was a rather young man with fair skin that matched his blonde hair—the only one wearing a tie. He was a handsome man and seemed out of place sitting with his peers.

Mary Ellen knew she was sitting in the hot seat before a row of church officers; nevertheless, she had decided to tell how the love of Jesus made a change in her miserable life. The sun-dried skin over Tom Hick's sharp cheekbones seemed to stretch and shine when she walked in the room. When she dressed earlier, she didn't intend to flaunt her feminine characteristics—just wanted to look her best. She was wearing a simple gray skirt and light, lavender sweater.

So far, the deacons sat silently with their eyes focused on Mary Ellen.

"After high school, this girl who was then an affirmed alcoholic, started working at Tony's Place on Vine Street to insure a steady supply of booze. Now gentlemen, let me tell you about a typical night at Tony's."

As she was talking to the five men, she would look at each of them full in the face—one at a time.

"This girl was now getting paid for what she did for free in high school. Her shift would begin around nine and continue into the wee hours. When a man approached her, she would decide yes or no—there were not many no's. The bar room was shaped like an L. Beyond the bar, in the short end of the L, was a small office. The mostly drunken girl would get up from her barstool and lead the man to the office to check into a room. With key in hand, he would go to his second-floor room by stairs near the front door. The girl would go to the second floor by stairs back of the office and enter his room. This girl wouldn't want to embarrass you by knowing the number of times those back stairs were used on a typical night."

A little weakness was diluting her boldness as she remembered those fifteen steps to the second floor. She then remembered that the Lord said in Hebrews 13:5, " . . . I will never leave thee nor forsake thee." With renewed power in her heart's engine, she looked at Hicks and then slowly moved her head until she got to the young man wearing a tie. Each could see her moistened eyes.

"Not one of you men, or any man, can understand or know about the life this girl was trapped in for over two years. Men, especially married men, wouldn't believe the gallons of tears that fell from this girl's smoke-dimmed eyes when she would try to go to sleep after . . . "

Mary Ellen tightened her lips to stop a flood of tears and regain her composure.

"And did you know the gutter has a basement—even a sub-basement. This girl who had just turned twenty was wallowing in a cesspool with zero ambition and with no hope to escape from endless pawing hands. But she did cope by staying numb drunk. She had seen enough living to earn a master's degree in Men-ology."

She had recovered and knew she would not cry. She was more determined to continue. She lowered her voice and announced, "I didn't get my degree because I dropped out of the 'College of Hard Knocks.' One blessed night, just before I lost my last ounce of sanity, Mason Dixon came to Tony's Place. Mason, the most decent man I have ever known, must have been sent by the Lord to rescue me. He asked me to go on a camping/fishing trip. He only came to Tony's to invite me to a new life. As soon as he left, a transition from bad to good started spinning in my confused head. I went on that overnight trip and experienced *clean* conversation and companionship for the first time in years." She emphasized 'clean.'

Her audience sat like stones except for some facial changes. Tom's cheekbones shined again a few times. She saw some rosy spots enlarge, and the skinny one's dark eyes seemed ready to pop out at times. Jerry frequently wiped perspiration from his bald head, and the young man in the fifth chair rapidly blinked his eyes and loosened his necktie.

From the time in her story about the 'College of Hard Knocks,' her volume had been increasing. Her ebullience was near boiling when she started to tell how Jesus picked her up from the gutter and restored her dignity and made her into a new person.

"Gentlemen. None of you can ever know from where I came—but thanks to Jesus and Mason, I am now part of this congregation and have been happy. I have been able to praise the Lord in the choir and show my thankfulness to him for forgiving *all*—I mean *all* of my sins. I have been reading my Bible, and there's a passage in Matthew 9:12 where Jesus said, '. . . *They that be whole need not a physician, but they that are sick.*'"

Mary Ellen stood and placed her hands on the back of the chair. She could feel a flush on her face.

"Well! Let me tell you that I was about as sick as a human could be. Jesus made me well when I repented of my many sins. Because of Him, I am now too blessed to ever again be sick and depressed. I know I'm still a young Christian but I'm learning to lean more and more on Him. He gave me courage and words today, and I know He will always be with me."

She thought it safe to catch a deep breath of much needed air. She knew her cheeks were rosy and the room seemed a lot warmer. The five statues before her were starting to move a bit. Two even turned their heads looking at the one beside them. It may have been the Holy fire in her eyes that caused them to squirm. But when she moved a step toward them, they all stood up.

"Gentlemen! You may have me removed from this congregation but no one—I mean *no one* can remove the love of Jesus from my heart and reverse the new life He gave me."

With a nod, Mary Ellen Dixon walked out of the room. She later heard that after a time of soul searching, Tom faced the others and reverently spoke, "Gentlemen, we need to have a meeting."

Those were the first words uttered by any of the deacons.

"Oh Robert, that is such a beautiful story." She stopped and hesitantly asked, "They surely didn't excommunicate her. Didn't you say she was still singing in the choir?"

"She's still there."

The following Sunday after the meeting, Tom Hicks went up front as soon as the service started. He didn't do this often, and the congregation took notice. He announced that a situation recently came to the attention of the deacon board. We decided to have a special meeting to address the problem for the good of the church.

The senior deacon stopped talking—most believed he was collecting his thoughts. The ones on the first few pews could see tears in his eyes but could also see that his tanned face appeared to be relaxed and supple with no tightness about his prominent cheekbones. During this brief interlude, he had slightly bowed his head. When he looked up, he hesitated again. Many in the congregation knew about last Monday's meeting but didn't know the deacons' decision. Mary Ellen had not been informed of anything and expected Tom to announce that for the good of the church the deacon board had decided to ask Mrs. Dixon to leave this congregation.

Tom straightened his small frame and declared in a humble manner, "Folks, I've been a deacon for thirty-two years and a Christian for much longer. In our special deacon's meeting last Monday, I rediscovered the saving power of our Jesus and the depth of his love. I realized that his blood can forgive all sins no matter how big or how many. Your deacons are more dedicated and better Christians and better servants of this congregation because of that meeting last Monday."

Tom stopped to wipe some tears from his eyes. Several people looked at Mary Ellen's angelic face as tears sparkled on their way to her lap. Apprehensions of the minute before was being washed down her face and replaced with an enhanced make-over of God's love. Tom continued with a greater conviction to deliver his renewed passion to the saving power of Jesus.

"They's a song our choir sings."

The pianist (by previous arrangement) started to play softly. Tom then turned to the direction of the choir.

"But this beautiful Sabbath day, I would like for Mrs. Mary Ellen Dixon to sing it as a solo." Tom abruptly sat down.

Surprised, Mary Ellen did not stand. Later, she said her heart actually felt like it was in her throat—she couldn't breathe. Even without oxygen, her mind remembered that she had told the deacons that Jesus would always be with her. She was beginning to wonder where He was when her foot moved. She then slowly and tearfully walked down from the choir loft and spoke to *her* church family.

"You all know I am a young Christian. This song is my testimony to the power of Jesus as I am learning more and more to lean on Him."

Robert and Mary sat silently for a while before he turned to her. "I was there and feel sure that 'Learning to Lean' has never been sung with more thanksgiving and acknowledgement to Jesus for changing a life. I don't think there was a dry eye in the church."

They again sat without talking for a minute or so until Mary asked, "Robert, what happened to—"

"Ah yes! What happened to Ollie? He and Sissy moved to St Louis six months later. Mason said Ollie told a deacon that he couldn't be part of a church that allowed a prostitute to sing in the choir. And also, Mary Ellen still talks with Sissy on the phone. She has said nothing that would indicate her knowledge about her husband's double life."

The rest of the trip to Burlington was a little lusterless for Mary as she often thought about the other Mary's changed life. She, like deacon Hicks, increased her love for Jesus after hearing specifically how all sins are forgiven. She also wondered if she would be counting stair steps and remembering how Ellen must have felt. She decided her mind could only dimly imagine the dread and shame that filled Mary Ellen's fuzzy mind during each ascent of those back stairs. Only a strong person could have endured the hopelessness she must have experienced during those two years. At that instant, Mary believed the Lord picked Mary Ellen to demonstrate that all sins can be covered with His saving blood. Mary also believed that Mason must have known the caterpillar worm, Ellen, would change into a beautiful Mary Ellen butterfly.

Mary whispered, as she intently peered through the windshield, "You know Robert? I wish millions could know about Mary Ellen's changed life."

"I know what you mean."

CHAPTER TEN

. . . unexpected hours together

A little past eleven, Mary's spinning head settled on her pillow. She had been up since six, and another day with Robert was now another sweet memory. The brunch that was cancelled last Saturday happily happened at ten today. She made a Danish Tea Ring that was enjoyed by all. She started at six because the yeast dough for the Danish had to rise two times. Robert had never tasted such a treat. It was chock-full of apples, raisins, pecans, brown sugar, cinnamon, and butter.

After the good food had sailed out of her mind, she remembered the times of ambivalence during the day. Those simultaneous feelings of joy and sadness each time she touched Robert. This was the last full day with him before he would fly away and leave her to return to pre-Robert days. But she knew her life would never be the same now that she had met him. She tried to organize the day's events to pacify and slow her whirling mind.

After brunch, they decided to sightsee with no schedule except to return in time for the dinner being prepared by Maureen. Freewheeling through beautiful Vermont was indeed delightful. Property owners took great pride in the appearance of their little slice of the state. Many hours of tender loving care was evident by creative landscaping that included colorful splashes of flowers. Artfully integrated in the designs were stones, shrubs, trees, and the flowers. From a distance, some yards looked like a mottled masterpiece.

Once, in a small town, she had remarked to Robert about all the tourists. She told him how, until now, she would resent them for crowding the streets and sidewalks. The Vermonters had endured a cold, snowy winter and when they got out to enjoy the warm sunshine, the tourists were in their face. Of course her attitude mellowed after working in a tourism office. But a definite change occurred when a certain West Virginian tourist crowded into her heart. The day was really great, despite the periods of melancholy because of his imminent departure. They just hung out and laughed about silly things—her tourist friend sure could make a Yankee laugh.

They went to the living room after dinner and returned to the dining room two hours later for more dessert. Maureen was still buoyant from compounded compliments about her dinner. When a good cook passes an accolade, it's special—Aunt Molly had been invited and wanted two recipes.

The two hours in the living room were a memory for all to cherish. With Robert at the piano, they had sung about every song written including all the Irish songs. Robert Arlington was a clean living young man with strong morals. But he did have a weakness—almost like an addiction. He loved to participate

in a sing-a-long. He had a pleasing voice, and his "Danny Boy" song was sensational. Mary's voice was low but pretty. Maureen was a soprano and could have attained some greatness had she trained. Aunt Molly probably enjoyed her singing more than the others. She was a little too loud at times, but when a song was finished, she had delivered the composer's expression plus some of her own embellishing expressions.

Mary was so proud of Robert's talent as she remembered the evening of music. She was also remembering kissing goodnight on the front porch. But it was more holding and clinging than kissing. Being about the same height, they interlocked like a jigsaw puzzle. Each had a wet shoulder from happy tears laced with sprinkles of sadness. Their beautiful time together would soon be a memory she couldn't hold in her arms.

As she tried to drift off to sleepy-land, her mind was both contented and apprehensive of the future. Last Friday morning before nine o'clock, she had her future planned. She was eagerly expecting a good job offer and felt this new phase in her life would lead to a successful career. Her goal, last Friday, was a job that would be the manifestation of the worthiness of all those long hours of study. It would be the reward for a deprived social life while she achieved excellence in the academic world.

It was all planned—she would start dating after she landed that good job. Her future plans were not so well mapped now as she heard the clock down stairs strike twelve times. Confusion began swirling in her mind along with contentment and apprehension. The press of time was a factor because Robert just suddenly walked into her planned life. She really did love him—he was even more than her dream man. But right now, she needed sleep.

Robert was at Mary's house early for a continental breakfast. They were in a jolly mood, but they both knew departure blues could not be mitigated with happy smiles. Maureen really seemed sad that Robert was leaving. She told him how glad she was to have met him and to please come back.

By the time they arrived at the airport, a sickening feeling was all over Mary. They had driven separate cars, and she couldn't remember her thoughts during the drive. The last five minutes of the two hours at the airport was a classical parting scene. They were alone in the crowd, recollecting and imparting their individual spin on unexpected hours together since last Friday. They were so thankful and yet mystified that fate set their hearts on a collision course. Robert's last words, as their fingertips lost contact, were his promise to see her soon. Mary was still feeling that last sensation of his warm fingers as she slowly walked to her car.

Losing her father was hard, but she had never experienced such emotional pain as now. She knew it didn't have to be permanent, but—gone is still gone. Her objective starting right then was to regain control of her senses and to stop by the tourism office to see Abby. She was going to first tell her about the fancy restaurant. Control started when she began laughing about his new clothes and the duct tape.

CHAPTER ELEVEN

. . . he had a big surprise for her.

Seated in the plane, Robert was staring but not seeing, listening but not hearing, and thinking but not comprehending. His dour expression wasn't indicative of his happiness a few minutes ago when he was holding a dream that had come true. Eddies of despondency were drifting in and out of his melancholy mind. His dispirited mood controlled him for many lofty miles. Some whirlpools of sadness were slowly replaced with glints of happy times with Mary. Happiness of mind compounded as he reviewed major events with her. He then realized that from the time he first heard her voice, he was falling in love with her. He tarried with the memory of holding her—all his dreams had come true.

A changing Robert Arlington tapped his fingers on his leg while he looked out the window. In a quick movement he found some paper and started writing.

Words and melody of a song merged together like magic. He simply relived time with Mary, beginning with the phone call. He could hear the piano playing in his mind. The melody started low, and the first three words were just a whisper—"When I first"—Then the words started waxing louder and the music higher in pitch—"heard your voice"—Then louder and higher—"it was like I had no choice." Then the fullness of his heart's desire was uttered for the whole world to hear—"I was falling in love with you." After eight measures of four-four time, the melody for the verses was established. He had written many songs, but none had been completed in twenty minutes.

The plane was cruising at 30,000 feet. Robert thought, "Maybe so for the other passengers." He was soaring at an empyreal attitude where long, flowing angel hair was softly brushing his face and bringing happy tears to his eyes. While writing the song, his senses were vaulted to a celestial realm nearly to the bar he sailed over during their first kiss. He didn't care who saw him wipe his tears before gingerly folding the piece of paper containing sixteen lines. The music was safely locked in his head to be retrieved when he would sit down at a piano.

What a difference a song can make! Robert's dour expression changed to the epitome of happiness as he contentedly went to sleep.

When he returned, Robert had dinner with Mason and Mary Ellen. He explained about Mary Bly O'Day, and thanked Mason for recommending the New England states. Robert stated that another trip would be necessary since only one state was visited. He didn't tell them that his next trip was already planned. A company training school to be conducted in Richmond, Virginia was scheduled months ago for the last week in September. He had decided to fly from Richmond to Montpelier on Friday after class. By taking off work Monday, he and Mary would have a wonderful weekend together.

In the excitement of seeing Mary again, Robert forgot to tell his mother about the return Vermont trip after the Richmond school. About the same time he was flying north to surprise Mary, she was flying south to surprise him. Since their last time together, they had only partially appeased their longing for each other with phone calls and letters.

Robert had already told Mary in a phone conversation that he had a big surprise for her. She tried to pry it from him, but he was steadfast and only teased her about it. She would know as soon as they could be together again. Of course it was the song, but Mary was thinking engagement ring. She had resolved in her heart that marriage was the ultimate conclusion to their chance meeting. When he inserted an enigma into their relationship equation, her desire to hold him grew. An impromptu plan was formulated. In a surprise appearance, she would invade his homeland and he would unconditionally surrender his heart to her and seal the pact with the engagement ring.

The sun rose and set according to predictable precision during the last week of August and the first three weeks of September. In anticipation of holding each other again, the weeks seemed like years to two young people so deeply in love. Because of the crescendo intensity of their desire to surprise, they could hardly breathe while dialing their respective calls from different airports.

Robert's mother, Jenny, said he was in Richmond, Virginia but would be home soon. Mary was cordially invited to come and wait for him—she was having baked chicken for supper.

Mary was really excited that she could surprise him by walking into the room and into his arms.

Mary's mother, believing Robert was calling from West Virginia, told him Mary should be landing in West Virginia in thirty minutes. She didn't know she was arriving unannounced.

Robert called home and talked to Mary. They had trouble finding words to explain the double surprise. Both would check if one could book a return flight within the next few hours. Forty-five minutes later, they reluctantly conceded to spend their special weekend apart. He had agreed to have brunch tomorrow with Maureen at Aunt Molly's. So for tonight, he would watch TV in the motel. He knew his mother would graciously entertain Mary.

After brunch, Robert walked outside. There was a chill in the air but plenty of sunshine. Aunt Molly's house and barn were situated on about three acres of level land. A hay field about the size of two football fields was between her house and the adjoining farm. A small house that seemed abandoned was located on the adjacent farm just beyond the hayfield. He walked over to look around. It was indeed empty, and one part of the back had fallen to the ground. The small front porch still had two rocking chairs as if waiting for someone to relax and enjoy the fresh September air. Near the front screen door was an old deteriorating bureau. Robert was looking at the rocking chairs when he heard his name. It was Tracy Evans, who was obviously glad to see him—alone. After fifteen minutes of persuasion, he agreed to attend a chuck wagon party that night. Tracy explained that it was just a group of young people having fun singing around the campfire. There would be no dating couples—just a bunch of guys and gals. She must have sensed not to come on too strongly to him and was implying that the party would be a generic gathering.

At six, Robert was at Tracy's house getting ready for what he perceived to be a sing-a-long. Two tired looking horses were hitched to a wagon piled high with hay. Five guys and four gals climbed onto the hay ready for some fun. Robert started singing as soon as they were moving.

By nine, the party's format was established. Robert and another boy and a girl were doing most of the singing. Tracy was right next to mad. Robert didn't know it, but the party was arranged after they met at the abandoned house. She had plans for them tonight that weren't about singing. Tracy's specifically designed party ended at ten on a sour note. She announced that blind people shouldn't stay out late—she started packing, and it was over.

Robert called home to tell Mary about the sing-a-long. His mother explained that she and Jesse had gone to the Presbyterian Church for the first night of square dancing lessons. They talked a little longer about why Jesse was out with his Mary. She was to call Robert at the motel after square dancing. He was more than disturbed about this news—he was angry. Jesse Lynn was his first cousin but not his first friend. They had spent a lot of time together at Pa Pa Lynn's farm while teenagers—especially during summer vacation. Jesse Monroe Lynn was Uncle William's son. William Thacker was Pa Pa Lynn's only son, a brother to Robert's mother, Jenny. During high school, Jesse was popular with the girls. He didn't look at all like Robert but was nevertheless handsome. His hair was curly and between brown and blonde. Probably his best *physical* asset was his quick smile and white teeth. But his absolute best overall asset was charisma. He truly had a special quality of leadership—that is—leading girls into his spidery snare with charming and flattering words.

After a girl was in his web, his forte was to love them and leave them. Robert only knew for sure of three high school girls with broken hearts that were left to flounder in Jesse's wake of lies. While he was innocently singing songs around a campfire, Mary was dancing with a greedy construction worker.

Robert's mother called her sister-in-law, Sara Beth Lynn, about the big mix-up with Robert and Mary wanting to surprise each other. Sara Beth mentioned this bit of news to Jesse. He assumed an obligation to entertain his cousin's friend while she was in a strange land.

Mary was so excited while telling Robert about the square dancing that he didn't get a chance to tell about the sing-a-long. She had never had so much fun. She enthusiastically explained that the "caller" would walk them through the movements before the music started. Her voice got louder when telling how the rhythm of the fiddle and banjo pulsated through her relaxed body. Without stopping, she told that groups of four couples would start in square formations. The caller would direct them to promenade, form a star, grand right and left, swing your partner and do-si-do. She laughed uncontrollably while telling how one man would often get lost and get in another foursome's group.

Robert interrupted. "Mary, I know how to square dance."

There was silence for a second or so before she gleefully responded, "Why dear, you didn't tell me you could square dance." She started laughing again.

"This man who got lost." Mary laughed almost hysterically while sputtering, "Someone . . . someone gave him a . . . " She again had to stop to laugh before finally crying out, "A compass!"

While she was still laughing, he quickly told her about the sing-a-long. She didn't seem disturbed that he was out with Tracy. She seemed to want to laugh and talk about what a good time they had in the church basement and how she enjoyed the snacks and punch.

Thinking about their conversation later, Robert became furious when remembering one of Mary's comments about being light-headed and dizzy. She attributed it to dancing round and round. But he knew exactly why she was dizzy—Jesse had spiked her punch with "moonshine" whiskey. He had known him to do this before to unsuspecting girls.

It was a long time before Robert went to sleep.

"That's all for now Ralph. That was a low time for me. The beginning of a period in my life I don't like to remember."

"Okay Robert, think about our next session. I need to know everything possible about Jesse. I know it's hard, but of course he's the reason we are talking. There wasn't much said at the trial about his character. Had I been your lawyer that would have been different. Michelle and I have . . . I mean we believe we know your character. Now Robert, please don't misunderstand my next—"

Robert interrupted by quickly saying, "Ralph! I know what you are going to say. You see—I've lived our last chapter together before this . . . this place. You don't have to question Mary's character."

"No! No Robert! I have not drawn any conclusions about Mary's character nor her loyalty to you. I deal in facts, plus I haven't read the last chapter. I don't know what happened after your flip-flop weekend.

The Next Day ✌

Ralph turned on the tape recorder as he watched Robert's eyes wander around the room. He saw eyes burdened with sadness—eyes washed by uncountable tears and still clouded from gritty sands of time. Sands of an unhappy period that had left him nearly blinded to any brightness in the future. Robert suddenly looked squarely at Ralph—his lips were pressed hard together. Slowly, he started talking and was barely audible.

"Two weeks after our mixed-up weekend, Jesse showed up on Mary's front porch. He got her address by snooping in my room one day while I was at work. She took him to meet Tracy—and left him there. Three days later, he was back on her porch."

Robert paused and looked up at Ralph. "Jesse is a determined person and gets what he wants. He quit his job in West Virginia, which was common for him. He could always get another job somewhere." Robert stopped again as if deciding just how to word his next statement.

"She did say she was impressed that he quit his job to be with her again, but then she didn't know his work habits.

The day she received notice about her first real job after college, Jesse reappeared at her house. Her job was teaching English to emigrants at Northeastern University, which is located near Boston. He persuaded her to let him help her move. He told her that he had a job waiting in Boston and would be glad to drive her to 'bean town.' They were together three days in Montpelier getting ready to move. Mary withdrew a large portion of her savings after finding that Jesse was a little short of cash. She was so thrilled about her job and appreciative that he was helping that she permitted him two goodnight kisses."

"How long did Jesse stay with Mary in Boston?"

Robert didn't answer.

"Did Jesse stay long in Boston with Mary?"

"Oh no! They got there in the afternoon and he left later that night."

Ralph was beginning to understand this Jesse guy. He was ready to ask if Jesse really had a job and paid back the borrowed money when Robert looked up with his lips pressed together again. After a deep sigh he said, "I may tell you later what happened."

Robert quickly stood and extended his hand. His face was stern and void of any discernable joy. It wasn't time for the session to be over, and Ralph did not extend his hand. They looked at each for what seemed like minutes before Robert sat down. Ralph had prevailed. Robert continued almost in a monotone.

"After Mary went to Boston, she stopped writing. We had been exchanging letters and cards two to three times a week and telephone calls on the weekends. I called and found out about Boston and Jesse. Maureen said she tried to stop her from being with him. Mary's reply was, 'Oh Mother, he's Robert's cousin and he's helping me move. He has a job waiting for him. It's only 'til I get into my apartment.' Maureen said Mary changed when Jesse came on the scene. I called and called until Maureen informed me that Mary said for me to stop trying to contact her.

My life was over. It was not easy, especially when Aunt Sara said she didn't know where Jesse was living. You can imagine what I thought."

Robert stood again while saying, "Mary should tell about Boston."

CHAPTER TWELVE

. . . it didn't sound like a good news call.

"Robert, do you know it's snowing harder?"

"Yes."

"Do you think Joyce Ann and Raymond will be going to their Christmas dinner?"

"Yes."

Robert's mother was still much concerned with his attitude and drab existence since he lost his Vermont girl. While watching large snowflakes lazily float and land on front yard shrubs, she tried to remember when Mary spent the weekend with her. With some cross-referencing of remembered events, she decided it was September '97. Since it was now a week before Christmas, a little mental arithmetic placed her visit fifteen months ago. Her son needed to find someone else and forget what he couldn't do anything about. At least that's how she summarized his sad situation.

"Here, let me help you."

Joyce Ann Bell handed the pearl necklace to her husband, Raymond. After the clasp was fixed, he walked in front of his wife of over sixteen years and looked at her for a moment.

"You're beautiful."

"Well thank you, kind sir."

After a slight pause,

"How many years have we been going to the Stephen Christmas party?"

"Oh . . . I don't know . . . Wait a minute, I was eight months along with Heather at the first one. That would be fifteen."

At this instant, Heather was passing by her parent's bedroom door and heard her name. She stopped at the partially opened door.

Raymond was looking at his watch as he asked, "Shouldn't Robert be here?"

"Oh, we have a little time."

Joyce Ann almost sang her answer, reflecting her excitement for the long awaited Christmas dinner. She was fidgeting with her blouse when the timbre of her voice changed.

"You know, I'm really worried about my brother's situation. It's been over a year since that girl. . ." She stopped and blankly stared in the mirror before continuing her concern about her brother. "He just works all the time. I don't think he goes anywhere except here. I wasn't sure he would come tonight—I sort of had to beg him."

Robert arrived right at six, keeping with his custom for punctuality. After discussing weather and road conditions for a few minutes, Raymond and Joyce Ann went out in the snow singing. Robert, Heather, and Charlie were soon settled comfortably in the family room. The room was spacious with a baby grand piano in a corner opposite the fireplace. Each seemed to be undergoing a transitional change from previous moods and thoughts. Robert was staring at the gas logs. Heather was alternately looking at the logs and at her Uncle Robert.

Charlie was stirring in a large game box between his feet. He abruptly asked, "Are we going to play in the snow?"

No one answered him.

"Are we going to play Monopoly tonight?"

No one answered him.

Heather was now looking at her Uncle Robert with a penetrating stare, as if trying to read his mind. He didn't seem to be aware of anyone else in the room. He watched the yellow and blue flames twist and curl as they leaped upward to vanish like his dreams. Of course the disappearing ragged blades of yellow heat were constantly being replaced with another blade and another one, and another one and . . . He closed his eyes. He had no more dreams. Nope, no more dreams. This Christmas season so far had been a bore. He had no spirit and didn't want any. He just wanted to work, and keep his mind busy with perplexing problems and challenging obstacles on the job.

Charlie sounded off again with enthusiasm common in twelve-year-old boys. "Come on, let's play Monopoly."

He didn't wait for a response, but instead placed the opened board on the coffee table.

Robert slowly moved his head and watched him count money for three players. He had played Monopoly many times with his niece and nephew—but not tonight. He was in no mood for a silly board game, and he didn't want to read to them, either. He had an uneventful day at work with too much time to think about things that he didn't want to remember. Many months ago he thought he could mask his true feelings from people around him. He had some success, but his counterfeit personality was definitely not working tonight.

During the short time Robert had been staring at the bouncing flames, Heather, with her head slightly bowed, fixed her eyes on her Uncle Robert. She finally got the courage to ask, "Uncle Robert," She hesitated while moving her head to look more directly at him, "Mother said tonight that she was worried about you."

She paused as if waiting for a reply. Through the months she had heard a little from her mother and grandmother about his past girl friend. After what she heard tonight, she was really curious. Quickly she asked, "How did you meet Mary, and what ever happened to her?"

He turned again to the gas logs. "What ever happened to Mary" ripped through his entire body like electricity. After the shock subsided, his mind suddenly changed from dispirited to neutral. His mind was totally blank for some period of time— he didn't know how long. Then in bits of perception, he pieced together a fuzzy fact that he had not heard from her for over a year. Slowly, he further realized something was happening in his tired, subconscious mind. A revelation he had avoided for months was stirring in a locked compartment of his memory. He was accepting that bad day in his life when Mary said to leave her alone.

Maybe what happened at work today was surfacing to mesh with Heather's question. Last June, a new girl entered his life—well sort of. Nicole Adkins, just out of college, started working in his section. They were together often. She was fun to be with, and he had even laughed some while together, but they had never dated. Today, she pointedly asked when they were going to have dinner together. He told her that he had to baby-sit tonight and didn't mention a later time to dine.

Instantly, after all these months, he painfully admitted to himself that it was over. Mary was gone. A strange feeling flashed through his body. He immediately sensed an unexpected relief. His façade seemed to have cracked and reality was seeping into his blurry mind. She's gone forever, so why not tell your niece. He jerked his head around to look at Heather. Her expression revealed that she was waiting for an answer.

"Heather."

He stopped while trying to convince his tight lips to say what had just migrated from his heart. Again he started.

"Heather."

He stopped again.

She looked at him as if to say, "Yes, go on."

"So you want to know how I met her. But first, just what did your mother say about me?"

"Ahh, well. . . that you work all the time, and it's been over a year since. . .."

Robert blurted, "Okay, okay that's right."

Charlie pleadingly asked, "Are we going to play Monopoly?"

Robert looked at him for a second or two. His mind was crowded with events of that first day with her. She was gone, but not her memories complete with sound, sight, and touch. He remembered the first time he heard her voice and the first time he looked into those beautiful eyes. Then later, the first time they touched finger tips.

With his eyes still fixed on Charlie, he softly answered, "No Charlie, something different tonight. I'm going to tell you two a story." Robert rotated the swivel rocker to look directly at Heather as he continued, "It's a story about the game of life. We won't be playing a board game."

He quickly glanced at Charlie, "All you have to do is listen. You don't even have to pass GO."

As Charlie was saying "shucks." He threw the dice and cried, "Wow! Two sixes, I would have gone first."

Heather, with her head tilted and slightly bowed, looked up at her Uncle and revealed a thin smile as her eyes glistened with a victorious glint. She really wanted to hear this story, especially all the romantic parts. Charlie moved back and curled up on one end of the sofa. Heather claimed the other end and tucked her legs beneath her. Robert briefly looked at his audience and then fixed his eyes on the dancing flames in the fireplace.

Joyce Ann had baked two apple pies and placed them on the counter just before he arrived. While removing his coat and snow in the foyer, he remembered similar kitchen scents in a house in Montpelier, Vermont. In addition to warm apple pie spices permeating his sister's house, there was also the Christmas tree and pine garland diffusing pungent seasonal oils into the warm room. Mingled with the warm, spicy pine air were also whiffs of vanilla from a dozen candles near the fireplace. He was feeling (the first time in months) a little like the other side of lonely. He could now think about her without pain and remorse. He had often blamed himself for the breakup, and had often thought he should have loved her more. In a mellowness of mind that had escaped him for so long, Robert Arlington was organizing a story plan about the happiest and saddest times in life.

"Okay my little ones, listen to a story about a man who went on a vacation in August 1997."

Smiles flashed on the youthful faces nestled on the sofa. They were hearing an ebullient uncle of a pre-Mary era.

"I had been working for two years with little time off. So I was ready for a vacation. Okay, okay it was Friday, August 15, 1997. I'll never forget that day. But wait, I need to back up 'bout three weeks. I called the Department of Tourism for each of the six New England States. They in turn sent me maps and books aplenty."

Robert looked directly at Heather. She didn't move her body or change her expression. In a tone reflective of a cherished memory, he answered her question.

"That's when I met Mary Bly, Mary Bly O'Day." He quickly added, "by telephone. Vermont was the sixth state I called."

Robert closed his eyes. He guessed this was the first time he had spoken her name for. . . he couldn't remember. He didn't feel like he was in danger of passing out, so he continued his story.

"I heard the sweetest voice say, 'Hello, may I help you?' At that instant, I connected somehow with her. We talked for over twenty minutes." He paused and looked at the ceiling for a few seconds. With eyes closed, a rush of pleasant thoughts cruised through his entire body.

"Ah yes, we talked over twenty minutes. Later, we couldn't remember all of the conversation, except weather and vacation stuff. Well, we did exchange names and occupations. I told her my specific plans about touring the six states. I was flying to Connecticut, getting a rental car and driving to Rhode Island, New Hampshire, Massachusetts, Maine, New Hampshire panhandle, and finally to Vermont. I would then turn in the car at the airport and fly back to West Virginia. You have probably figured out that there wouldn't be much time for sightseeing. Guess you could call it a windshield vacation."

Charlie waved his hand, "What is your occupation?"

"Well Charlie, I'm an electrical engineer working for the Power Company in Huntington."

Charlie seemed satisfied as he nodded his head.

"Okay where was I, oh yes. . .," He lowered his head and locked his hands together. With an imperceptive smile on his tanned face and with deep seriousness, he continued.

"A week after I talked with Mary Bly, I made a major decision. I was going to Montpelier first."

Charlie broke in. "Now where is that?"

"Vermont." Heather quickly answered.

"I wanted to see her really bad. I couldn't get her off my mind—day and night. I didn't even know if she was engaged or married. I didn't know if she would be there. When we talked, she was working part-time at the tourism office. I did know she had just received her master's right after her undergraduate's degree. So I had an idea about her age."

Robert stared at the fireplace, seemingly unaware of anyone else in the room. He didn't speak for quite a long time. Then with a quiver in his voice he slowly announced, "It was Friday. . . August 15, 1997."

The phone rang five minutes past midnight. Charlie was asleep on the sofa. Robert heard it, thinking Joyce Ann was calling. His mind was mellow since he had decided to have a happy Christmas with Nicole. The past months were suddenly a manageable memory. Months ago, his mother told him to do something about his love for Mary or forget her and move on with his life. His mother's advice was always tucked in the back of his mind, but it wasn't until tonight that he finally concluded Mary did not want him. It was over. Tonight, enough of her memory had spun from his mind to permit a forward look without her.

Heather answered the phone in the kitchen.

"Uncle Robert! Uncle Robert!" She excitedly repeated, "Uncle Robert! It's Mary! Can you believe it? It's her."

The contentment he had generated by erasing Mary from his mind changed to a nervous twitch throughout his body. This had happened in one giant, jerky leap. He thought, "Could my emotions stand this stretch?"

While staring at the fire, a thousand thoughts flooded his numbed mind. Most of his senses had been shorted by the bolt of lighting that had zigzagged through his ears when he heard her name. He had only fainted once after a snow-sledding accident and that same "losing it" feeling was happening again.

"Uncle Robert! She wants to talk to you."

In slow motion, he walked to the phone. The few steps must have started enough blood circulating in his brain for him to speak in a near normal voice.

"Hello, this is Robert."

He heard crying—it didn't sound like a good news call. He next heard strained words dripping with tears.

"Robert . . . Hi . . . Robert, I'm sorry to call so late."

Her voice was soft and still "Yankee"—and still sweet. He suddenly couldn't breathe. He was reverting back to the fainting feeling but was saved when she spoke again.

"How have you been? I mean . . . Oh Robert . . . I'm so sorry. I've . . . I had some things to work out in my life."

"Mary! Are you sick?"

"No, no, I'm not sick. I have wanted to call so many times, but it has just now worked out with the Lord's help."

Robert couldn't say anything as he heard her crying again.

"Robert, I have missed you so much. I'm still in Boston. I just called Mother and . . . "

There were several seconds of silence. Interspersed with sobs and sniffling he heard, "I'm going back home today."

At this instant, he knew banked embers of Mary's memory were beginning to sparkle from his increased breathing rate. He couldn't fully grasp the significance of her statement. He had assumed she was at home or near home these past many months.

Heather walked to his side and whispered, "Is she okay?"

Robert bobbed his head up and down.

After meeting Mary when she was here over a year ago, she liked her and was sad when they parted. She was really happy for Uncle Robert after hearing more about her tonight.

"I'm leaving around nine later today. Did you hear I'm still in Boston?"

Robert didn't immediately answer—and then, "Did you say today?"

"Yes, I'm going back home today." Robert didn't say anything. "Oh Robert, I wouldn't blame you if you hung up—I wanted to call sooner."

"Did you say you are going back home today?"

"Yes! Yes! I've been so lonely—I have so much to tell you."

"You say you're not sick. Have you been sick?"

"No, no, I've just been lonely and couldn't call sooner."

"Why?"

"I want to tell you. That's why I'm calling."

He heard some more sobs. He then told her that he had also been lonely for many months without any word from her. They talked a few minutes longer—he asked about her job—she asked about his job. He thanked her for calling and wished her a Merry Christmas. Then, the call was abruptly over. Thinking about the conversation later, he couldn't remember if he had mentioned the snow.

Before Robert could recover from the unexpected phone call, the phone rang again. He answered and it was Joyce Ann calling about the heavy snow—they couldn't drive back home tonight. He agreed to stay overnight with Heather and Charlie. Before the phone was cradled, he asked Heather if she wanted more pie. If she noticed a change in Robert's enthusiasm, she didn't show it. After talking about the snow and road conditions and the call from Mary, Heather announced she was going to bed.

She asked while leaving the room, "Are you going to call Mary?"

Robert didn't answer. She turned around and looked at him in a way that demanded an answer. He smiled and said, "I might just go see her before Christmas."

Robert had many thoughts while sitting alone watching flames dancing about the gas logs. She had told her mother that she was coming back home today, and she had so much to tell him. He couldn't say that about his life. Not much to tell her about himself. His routine hadn't varied much the past year— just depression and working a lot.

His mind kept recycling what she said about "coming home today." It suddenly struck a jubilant chord in his happy mind. He sat down at the piano.

CHAPTER THIRTEEN

"I asked Jesus to forgive me . . .

Ralph called Michelle after he arrived home from prison. They talked about the rental business before he told her Mary would be at his office at nine tomorrow morning. She seemed a little preoccupied after he told her Mary would be telling about her time in Boston. He wanted to ask if he could come over tonight—but didn't and went to bed in a disconsolate mood. It seemed he would never get to kiss her. She had shared some of her personal life with him, but he wondered if it could be more.

Mary entered the office a few minutes before nine. Ralph had talked with her on the phone, bringing her up to date with Robert's last part of the deposition. This morning she seemed relaxed and ready to continue her part. Before Ralph turned on the recorder, she complimented Michelle on her pretty dress and the natural beauty of her long hair. Ralph looked at Michelle and nodded in agreement.

"I agree." As he looked at her, he thought, "I should have said that first." He then asked Mary, "Tell us about Boston and when you returned to live with your mother."

"First, let me begin a week before Christmas 1998.

I can never forget the date—the nineteenth. I experienced months of depression and long, sleepless nights before calling Robert from Boston a little past midnight that day. It took months trying to decide what to do with my messed-up life. After going to Boston, Mother and I talked by phone often. I even went back home for a weekend a month after I left." Mary looked out the window for a few seconds. "I stopped calling home soon after that visit. I was so ashamed. I didn't want any contact with family or Robert. That's when I disconnected my telephone."

She stopped talking and looked at Michelle and then to Ralph and back to Michelle. Her face glowed with a grimacing blush that Michelle took to be embarrassment. Looking straight at Ralph, she laboriously pushed out some guilt-coated words after a deep breath.

"I had a baby while in Boston."

Michelle glanced at Ralph. The room was silent for several rapid heartbeats. Ralph broke the silence with low, soft words.

"When did Robert know about the baby?"

"He didn't call me back after my call on the nineteenth, but he called Aunt Molly and arranged a surprise visit on the twenty-third. I guess he thought it safe to surprise me this time. I doubt I can explain . . . "

Ralph and Michelle looked at each other with compassion while Mary recovered.

"It was a fantastic reunion. Aunt Molly came at six on Christmas Eve to see me. She was glad I was back home, but she and Mother rather quickly went to the kitchen. I sat down on the sofa watching the fire. As the flames disappeared up the chimney, I was beginning to wonder if my dreams were also disappearing. After the baby was born, I had some really hard times. I doubt you know what I'm talking about."

Mary hesitated and Ralph looked at Michelle. Understanding was dripping from her face. She went to Mary and embraced her.

"I understand about your hard times—I've been there too," she whispered.

There was a short period when they were holding up each other.

"I asked Jesus to forgive me and He did. And in my heart, I knew Robert and I would be together again. I was burning to tell him all about Boston. It was a couple of minutes before Robert walked into the room. I almost fainted. He hadn't called and now he was only a few feet away—smiling. Mother and Aunt Molly stayed in the kitchen. Did I say that was a fantastic reunion? We were soon nestled on the sofa before the fireplace. That was my best ever Christmas Eve up to that time."

Mary had attended some type of school most of her life. When she received the job offer, the elation was so great that good judgment took a backseat. When Jesse reappeared, caution also was repositioned. She was entranced with his wild manner—so different from Robert's honorable and conservative personality. Jesse was more daring and made her feel exhilarated with all the adventurous things he did and talked about. He had quit his job just to be with her. That had really impressed her.

Her furnished apartment wasn't great but would suit her needs. In gratitude for his help, she had permitted two quick kisses. Jesse's format for full compliance with his conquest of a woman included four steps: First, a kiss; and then an embrace; then caressing; and finally he expected and usually received full surrender. Mary didn't permit the embrace. Her new job was her focus, and Robert was her first and only love. Her deep-seated endeavors and thoughts were all for him. Jesse didn't always attain total conquest quickly and was patient when necessary.

It didn't take long to transfer her things from the car to the apartment. It was dinner after that. Jesse paid for the meal with money she had loaned him. Back at the apartment Mary soon announced that it was time for him to leave. She was tired and needed to go to bed. That was her plan. His plan was to stay in the apartment with her. He reminded her that it was raining and cold and could he please sleep on the sofa just for the night.

He had tried to embrace her only once two days ago. Since then he had been respectable and courteous. She caved in when looking into his begging eyes.

Two hours later, she awoke looking into his eyes, which were glazed with desire. She fought with all her strength, but he was too powerful and too determined. Before the humiliation, shame, and guilt consumed her, she found some residual strength to put him out of the apartment. The reality of being raped the first night away from home was almost more than she could endure.

Hard work and new horizons were part of her Irish heritage. So with bundles of energy, Mary O'Day attacked her new job. She had pushed the Jesse episode from her mind until she knew for sure that she was pregnant.

Dear Reader:
Here's what Mary told Robert on Christmas Eve 1998:

"Robert, I wish you could just half way feel the happiness and thankfulness that is rushing throughout my body and mind. I have experienced some unexpected events since we were last together. Without the Lord's help, I would not be in your arms this most special night."

She looked more directly at him.

"And without you—I would not be a Christian. Oh Robert, I know the Lord sent you to me."

She lowered her head while Robert moved his head in the direction of the fireplace.

"Robert, you know Jesse came here right after our mixed-up weekend. I am so sorry and ashamed for what happened. I hope you will believe that I didn't see a storm coming. The exhilaration of my first job must have blinded me to his predatory nature. He exploited my foolish lack of worldly wisdom and plundered my naive innocence. All his moves were selfishly calculated to capture his prey—which was my body clutched in his devious claws. He was so nice and helpful getting me into my apartment. He lied to me about having a job waiting in Boston. I wrote a little poem about him. Want to hear it?"

Before Robert had a chance to answer, she recited it.

> *"True intentions so hard to tell,*
> *Liars should wear a tinkling bell.*
> *Innocent ears before mistakes,*
> *Could hear the storm before it breaks."*

"Mary, I knew all about Jesse and blame myself for not warning you after that square dance thing. But at that time, you didn't indicate any problem."

"Oh no Robert, it was all my fault. I wish that somehow I could tell young girls to steer clear of men like Jesse. I should have realized his nature, but I didn't because of my ignorance."

Mary lowered her head again and wiped some tears that suddenly appeared. From an answered prayer, she summoned the courage to continue.

"Robert." There were more tears before she boldly said, "Robert, he raped me."

Mary then turned to the the best man in the world sitting beside her.

"He stole a part me I was saving for you."

Robert's mind and eyes were fixed on the fire. He knew she had a baby and before a minute ago, had believed the conception was consensual. Maureen called his mother the next day after Mary called him and told her about the baby. Her suspicion was right because Mary had severed their friendship. Robert's mother told him about the baby so he would know what to do next.

When Mary told him to forget her, he knew something unexpected had happened. Within his most unhappy thoughts, he believed she had somehow become involved with Jesse. Even so, he loved her so much that he was willing and ready to forgive her. But after weeks, and months, and then a year of no contact, he decided to forget her. When she called, all those months of depression evaporated as he heard her voice.

Robert turned to Mary. Her face was flushed and more beautiful than any other time he could recall. With words full of honesty, he declared to his lovely Mary, "I love only you and nothing past, present, or future can come between us. I can't see how my happiness could be more complete than right now."

He gently placed his hands on her face and tenderly kissed her beautiful lips as she started to cry.

"Oh Robert, I don't deserve you. I wouldn't blame you if you got up and walked out of my life after you hear what I'm going to say next. I . . . I . . . have a baby. I conceived the first time."

After a few seconds, which seemed like an hour to Mary, he rose and motioned to her to also stand. He extended his arms and she rushed to him. She clung to him like a drowning victim. In soft sincere words, "May I see your baby?"

"Oh my lovely, shining knight, I have so much to tell you."

Maureen whispered to Molly when she heard the stairs creak. "Let's get out the refreshments."

The festivity in the O'Day house was truly a time of feasting and celebration. Maureen and Molly had prepared delicious food, and her daughter was back home and back with Robert. He eased over to the piano after the happy eating time. They all agreed later that Christmas carols never sounded better. After the sing-a-long, it was agreed that Robert and Molly would be staying all night due to the heavy snow.

Robert went back to the piano and announced that he had a special song to sing. He played a few chords and then turned around to address his audience.

"This song was going to be a surprise when I came to Vermont the weekend Mary went to West Virginia."

He told them how he was inspired to write the song on the plane back home after meeting Mary and then dedicated "Falling in Love" to Maureen's beautiful daughter.

Falling in Love

1. When I first heard your voice,
It was like I had no choice.
I was falling in love with you.
When we touched finger tips,
In my heart, I really knew
I was falling in love with you.

Chorus:
Through long nights, I have dreamed
I would find someone to love.
Then you came to me from above.
Holding you takes my breath
For my dreams have all come true.
I am falling in love with you.

2. What a sweet first embrace,
I was such a hopeless case.
I was falling in love with you.
When we kissed, time stood still
And my life began anew.
I was falling in love with you.

Chorus:
Through long nights, I have dreamed
I would find someone to love.
Then you came to me from above.
Holding you takes my breath
For my dreams have all come true.
I have fallen in love with you.

Mary was the first to speak after a long silence.

To Robert, her voice sounded like an angel might sound.

"Come over here Robert. I will fly away if I move. I have never felt so close to Heaven."

He securely locked his arms around his angel to keep her earthbound and said he now had a little story to tell.

He calmly told them what happened after Mary's phone call last week. He told how his heart soared to new heights—even into angel territory. With his face glowing from a dreamy smile, he asked Mary, "Do you remember what you said to your mother?"

Not waiting for an answer, he increased the brilliance of his smile and repeated her words. "Today, I'm coming back home."

Mary cried, "Yes I did, and I'm so glad."

Robert then told them about Heather and Charlie and that he was sitting with them when Mary called.

"Okay folks—after they went to bed, I think I was in Heaven for awhile. I was transitioned to another dimension. I must have been coated with comet dust or something for I was so inspired that I composed another song."

Robert walked back to the piano and played and sang his second song titled "Today."

Today

1. Today, there are rainbows glowing everywhere.
Thank you Lord for hearing my prayer.
Late last night, you were so alone.
You cried on the phone.
No more tears, you are coming home today.

Chorus:
So many times, I have prayed to again hear your voice.
My glad heart leaps with joy as I now rejoice.
Soon you'll be in my arms again,
I don't care where you've been.
By God's grace, you are coming home today.

2. When you called, there were Angels singing in my heart.
For you said we would never more part.
Lonely tears flowed day and night,
Joy was out of sight.
No more tears, you are coming home today.

Chorus:
So many times, I have prayed to again hear your voice.
My glad heart leaps with joy as I now rejoice.
Soon you'll be in my arms again,
I don't care where you've been.
By God's grace, you are coming home today.

When he finished, everyone, including Robert was crying. Three of the four present wanted to hear it again.

The two young ones then spent some time on the back porch watching snowflakes silently float down. The cold air helped them to mellow some after the warm feelings just generated in the house. While holding each other, they peered through the snowflakes toward Heaven and thanked Jesus aloud for their being back together.

Back on the sofa, Mary spoke first. "Oh I have so much to tell you. I didn't know what was going to happen when I knew for sure about the baby. There were days when my guilt and shame drove me to dangerous depths of despair. I was too ashamed for you and Mother to know. In the beginning, I believed you would not want to see me again, and I didn't even ask Jesus to forgive me. It was my fault that this happened because I let myself get into a vulnerable situation. I was coping, but it was hard. It was really hard until I met Alice—Alice Johnson. Suddenly one night at the University, I met her. Actually, she introduced herself to me and we became good friends."

Mary paused and looked at the fireplace as if to gather thoughts for her next statement. "Alice was so nice and helpful— sure did hate to leave her."

Mary paused again before continuing with more excitement in her voice. "When you were holding the baby, remember I said I would tell you why his name is Lynn Sean?"

"Yes, I've been wondering why Lynn?"

"Okay Robert dear, you shall know. It was during my seventh month when I had two glorious revelations."

She patted her heart.

"I almost lose my breath when I think about this. You know the story about Mary and Joseph and how Jesus was a Son of the Holy Spirit?"

"Yes . . . it's in Matthew and Luke."

"Okay! You know Joseph was not the father of Jesus. God was the father. Now hear this—I had a college course that included the chemistry of the blood. Here's a key characteristic in the miracle of birth—all birth. Not one drop of blood passes from mother to baby. Not one drop. Blood is produced in the developing embryo only after the male sperm is united with the female egg. The mother provides nutrients to the fetus for the production of blood but it's the male sperm combining with the female egg that creates blood. The bloodline is of the male. Little Lynn has a bloodline through your Uncle William and to Pa Pa Lynn. Had you been the father, the bloodline would not have been to your mentor—Pa Pa Lynn."

Tears were cascading down Mary's happy face.

"Oh my dear Robert! Even with all the bad I have endured, isn't the Lord so good?"

"My dearest Mary, the Lord is good. We don't always understand his ways. One of my favorite Bible verses is Romans 11:33." He reverently quoted the verse.

> *"O the depth of the riches both*
> *of his wisdom and knowledge of God!*
> *how unsearchable are his judgments,*
> *and his ways past finding out!"*

"Robert." Mary wiped more tears before she could continue. "You are so good and I can't thank the Lord enough that you waited for me."

Robert was crying now—but he confessed, "Mary, love of my heart, I had no choice."

"I had no choice either—love of my heart."

Mary lowered her head as more tears soaked her handkerchief. Neither was counting the seconds or minutes as two thankful hearts were making room for a rush of happiness that must have been sent from above. When she turned back to Robert, her eyes glistened and a few straggling tears trickled down her flushed face. She focused on him with an intensity that was almost hypnotic.

Then in words soft as an angel's whisper, "Robert, also in my seventh month, I knew we would someday be together again—remember I mentioned two revelations. Let's hope I don't fly away before you know what happened.

It was Saturday morning when this revelation started. I didn't get up from bed until after nine. I tried to sleep a lot so days wouldn't be so long and lonely. I had severed contact with everyone back home except writing to mother two or three times a month. My spirits had been ratcheting up since the realization about Pa Pa Lynn's bloodline. I was happy about that but was disconnected from a clear direction for my life."

Mary closed her eyes to pick the next words to say.

"You were constantly on my mind, but I was too ashamed to think about us together again. The Lynn bloodline was troubling me—without you it wouldn't mean anything. But that Saturday morning was different from all others before and since. I was elevated to a dimension way above my unusual, moody, dispirited, lonely existence and by eleven o'clock, I had formulated a joyous plan for the day. It was a remarkable plan. Maybe it was more insane than remarkable but I was driven to complete it. I didn't have much money but was going to splurge on expensive ingredients and prepare a special meal."

She waited for a comment. When Robert didn't speak, she asked, "Are you listening?"

"Yes, yes. Was your friend Alice dining with you?"

Mary restarted her story as if she didn't hear his answer to her question.

"I was tingling with delight . . . with joy . . . with a . . . with a spiritual feeling that crowded out all my anxieties and replaced them with a heightened expectation of a celebration—a jubilee. It was like before a child's birthday party or before Christmas.

Robert, I may have trouble telling this. I doubt I can halfway convey to you the celebration that happened in my small kitchen."

While Mary stopped for a breath, Robert asked again, "Did Alice dine with you?"

"No. You need to hear the rest. Okay, I went shopping and then prepared a meal that would make a gourmet chef jealous. She twisted a quick smile edged with pride before revealing her menu. She repeated it slowly seemingly remembering each preparatory step.

> *Asparagus soup with smoked chicken bits, black bread. Spinach salad with toasted hazelnuts and Dijon vinaigrette. Broiled veal chop, fingerling potatoes, braised swiss chard, apple chutney and crispy polenta garnished with sun dried tomatoes. Coconut crème pie was the finale."*

If Robert was impressed with the menu, he didn't communicate it to Mary. He couldn't have known the enthusiasm and vivacity she experienced planning, gathering ingredients, and preparing the meal. For the first time in nearly seven months, she was really happy that special Saturday and encouraged that her future was going to be brighter. Robert finally made a comment.

"Sounds like a grand meal, but I don't understand why you did it, and you still haven't said who dined with you. It must have been someone special."

Mary had a layered glow on her pretty face as she wiggled out of his arms and stood in front of the fireplace. The glow on her face seemed to sparkle as she continued her seventh month story.

"Robert . . . I . . . I know what happened. That day came from God. I was so happy and sure of my actions except for one thing. Five minutes after the table was set, I saw two place settings." She waved two fingers.

"I had set the table for two. It took a little while before I decided to leave the table as set. I know now it was all in God's plan, for indeed a special guest came that day. Now don't think me crazy, for my special guest was you."

Robert's expression quickly changed to surprise. Before he could counter her declaration, she waved her hand.

"I only put food in my plate and slowly enjoyed a most delightful meal. Contentment was all over me for a change. I had no idea where this was going. During the meal, I did often look across the table and see you . . . in my heart."

Mary paused and smiled. "I even saw you in your new clothes when we had dinner that most special night."

Robert couldn't keep from smiling too. Until now, he had been listening intently. The mention of his new pants with the duct tape improvisation brought a little relaxation, but he still didn't fully understand the significance of this story.

"Yes, I did laugh some but was mostly just blissfully peaceful. After the meal, it was all so clear—my feelings, the meal, and—are you ready for . . . for the dance? We danced and danced. Robert dear, it was so wonderful. Can you imagine how ashamed and guilty I felt for being alone in Boston without you and family? But not so that Saturday. I could feel your arms around me as we waltzed to 'The Loveliest Night of the Year.' You know the song. Ah yes, I was in love and was sure my feet were not touching the floor. I had never felt so intense but also relaxed at the same time. We could have been on an acre size ballroom as we waltzed around and around my tiny apartment. I was removed from the present to a . . . a place of beauty . . . and . . . and tranquillity . . . or maybe it was all an apparition.

But I know one thing for sure; clarity suddenly filled my being. All of my feelings and emotions of shame and desire for happiness were corralled and condensed into one crystal clear drop of discernment. There was instantly a great gulf between shame and desire. Happiness can't be meaningful if mingled with doleful swatches of shame. In an instant, happiness moved to the driver's seat in my life. We were going to be together again. I knew it in my heart, body, and soul."

Pausing and looking away from Robert, Mary repeated those beautiful words, "We were going to be together again."

She was still standing at the fireplace when delivering her proclamation. After a few seconds, she sat beside Robert on the sofa. He was beginning to feel her excitement and revelations of that day.

"Please don't think I lost my mind that beautiful day—I really just found some missing pieces. When my reconstructed mind reconnected with my thumping heart, I sat in my rocking chair for a long time—it took awhile for the tingling to subside. I should have called you then or sent a letter. But even after my beautiful trip to understanding land, I still couldn't ask you to come to Boston and get your girl friend that was seven months pregnant. I decided to have my precious baby in Boston, mostly because Alice Johnson was there to help me."

Mary fixed her eyes on a table lamp. She had delivered her say and was now ready to get in step with Robert's plans and march into a bright future. With her eyes still on the lamp, she spoke in dreamy words. "Remind me to tell you more about Alice."

Robert didn't answer. He was content to have Mary beside him again.

"Well dear Robert, you could never know how many times I have thanked our Lord for you. Nor could you know how many times I have prayed for your safety. Hold me tight before I fly away."

There were kisses that sent reunited hearts to unmapped regions of blissfulness—kisses that were steeped in the warmth of God's love and served in an overflowing cup of His promises.

"Well that's all for today. Remembering that Christmas Eve and Christmas Day have been a big reason for me to keep going on with my sad life after this awful thing. That memory and little Lynn have gotten me this far. But before I met you, Mr. Fenny, I had no hope that Robert could ever be freed."

Mary looked directly at Ralph who was now standing.

"What is your defense plan? Do you have any new evidence?"

Ralph didn't answer.

After a few embarrassing heartbeats, Michelle looked at him. "May I?"

"Oh sure...yes."

"We have an idea but no positive proof yet. We need a little more information about Jesse before we know for sure."

Ralph's heart was ready to explode—how he wanted to hold Michelle and kiss her and ask her if she would marry him. He had nothing to encourage Mary. Michelle saved him. She had one theory but not enough evidence even to mention it to Ralph. He had not thought of any way to free Robert.

The attorney at law and his helper sat in silence for a long time after Mary left.

CHAPTER FOURTEEN

He would soon tell the world . . .

Michelle was in Ralph's kitchen when Mary entered the office. Before she reached his desk, Michelle entered the room and screamed.

"Oh! Oh! Oh, let me hold him."

Mary beamed with a mother's pride as she handed Lynn to her. It would be five minutes before they finished with their mother/child dialogue. Ralph didn't want to say what was on his mind but sternly said, "Mary, I have reviewed the court transcript several times and there's no testimony to suggest that anyone other than Robert shot Jesse. I know it's all circumstantial. And also, you didn't have much to say."

"Well, Mr. Fenny, I answered the questions asked. Some of what I told the police wasn't mentioned at the trial."

"What! What did you say?"

"No, not all of it. I was so afraid that the baby would be used as evidence to convict Robert that I only said as little as possible."

Ralph remembered the police report and didn't know of any conflict with court proceedings.

In soft, courteous words he asked Mary to tell everything she told the police.

Michelle was still holding baby Lynn.

Robert and Mary went to visit Aunt Molly while on one of his trips to Montpelier. As soon as they arrived, she asked Robert to scare off the crows in the backyard. He got her husband's 12-gauge, double-barreled shotgun, and he and Mary walked to the back door. A big tree was nearly black with the birds. Just outside the door, he fired two shots and reloaded. He had only fired one more shot when they heard a loud noise that sounded like a gunshot from the direction of the abandoned house on the Tracy Evans property. They didn't move—just looked in that direction until they heard a cry for help.

Robert still had the shotgun in his hand when he arrived at the abandoned house. Mary had gotten there first. The front porch of the house faced away from Aunt Molly's house and when Robert got to the porch, Mary had Jesse's head cradled in her lap. He had been shot in the chest and by the size of his wound, it must have been from a shotgun. By the blood on the old bureau, it seemed he had collapsed and slid down the front of it to the floor. His left leg was twisted underneath him.

Ralph stopped Mary with a hand wave.

"Mary, all of what you just said is in the police report."

"I know that's what I told the two policemen."

"You said there was more."

"Yes. I was ready to tell you what Jesse said just before . . . "

Ralph apologized with a sheepish grin and a nod.

Mary finally forced out some tear-filled words. "He had lost a lot of blood, and I thought he was already gone when I asked, 'Who did this?' He half opened his eyes and whispered, 'Will you forgive me?' I immediately said, 'Yes I forgive you.' He then took his right hand and placed it on his left fingertips to form a "T" just before he . . . he died. Robert and I both knew he meant thanks."

Ralph glanced at Michelle as his mind focused on the scene described by Mary.

While getting baby Lynn from Michelle, she said in a conclusive tone, "You know the rest. Robert was still holding the shotgun when the police arrived. They were only a mile away when someone called."

Just like yesterday, the room was quiet after Mary left. Ralph and Michelle didn't look at each for a long time. They were replaying Mary's words. Then, simultaneously, they blurted each other's name. Ralph bowed after some smiles.

"Okay Ralph, we may have something here."

"What do you mean, dear?"

He actually blushed. It just seemed natural to say "dear." Michelle must have thought so, too, because she didn't react in any way as she expanded her thought.

"Until now, all we had were hours of romance between them, but there must be something useful from what she just said about forgiving a dying man."

Not giving her time to continue, Ralph interjected.

"I agree. There must be a clue the police left out we can trace."

Michelle screamed, "What did you say?"

"Well, the police left—"

"No! No! Before that—the part about a clue."

Ralph was puzzled with a grimace on his face as if searching for a clue to what she wanted.

"Ralph! You said we need a clue to—"

She walked closer to him and bolted, "A clue to *trace*."

Ralph's mouth flew open before he whispered, "Tracy . . . "

Ralph leaped over to Michelle with arms reaching. They grasped hands and started laughing and dancing around. After one rotation, he gleefully confessed, "I love you!"

After another turn, Michelle confessed without laughing, "I love you too!"

They stopped and looked at each other. Ralph started to tremble. He could feel an attraction to her stronger than any emotion that had ever coursed through his mind or body. Shy, timid Ralph Fenny became a new person when Michelle's next five soft words connected with his fluttering heart.

"Have for a long time."

Angels with the "Celestial Bureau of Kisses" would have to carefully check the glory mark for this kiss. Records can be broken.

Ralph was troubled as he sat in the Charlotte, North Carolina motel. He should have been happy and dancing for the recent change in his life. He and Michelle were in love. It was a love that couldn't be measured on any earthly scale. They loved and respected each other in a way that was greater than physical attraction. It was spiritual. He still trembled with an avalanche of glorious feelings when holding her. His heart would almost burst with admiration for her. He had never known anyone so wonderful. When holding her, he knew his arms were surrounding the manifestation of Jesus' love. He had never made a public profession about his belief in Jesus, but in his heart he knew that Jesus died for his sins. He would soon tell the world how much he loved Jesus.

He should also be happy about the new evidence that Michelle found. But he knew what Mary said about the "T" would not be acceptable in court. He had to have a confession from Tracy. That was why he was in a Charlotte motel, and he was dreading to confront her.

It took three days to locate her, and he had spent another two days learning her habits. Everything had to be done right, or Robert's chance for freedom would be lost. In the end, Ralph used the front door approach. He was waiting for her when she arrived at her apartment after work and told her about Jesse's dying statement.

Tracy had some faults, but she also had a conscience. She knew Robert was serving a life sentence for something she did. Ralph told her about some incriminating evidence he had on Jesse that could be in her favor. She confessed.

Five months after Tracy confessed, Robert Lynn Arlington was a free man, and her mother died two days after his freedom. Tracy's mother had been sick for over a year, and she was home from Charlotte to visit her when she shot Jesse. He had found her in Charlotte where she was working in the office of a construction company. She repeatedly told him that she never wanted to see him again, but he followed her to Vermont that fateful weekend. She agreed, after an argument, to meet him at the abandoned house. He had caused her painful hardships, and she was dangerously angry with him.

She entered the house by a side door and shot through the front screen door with a 12-gauge shotgun. She was also angry with Mary for introducing Jesse and didn't care when Robert was accused.

Tracy placed all the blame on Jesse when she found out she was pregnant. The attraction—not love—she had for him turned to hate. Her world of fun-loving living quickly turned up side down. She made a bold decision and relocated to Charlotte. For the hard times of grief and loneliness, she was blessed with a beautiful baby girl.

@ *The End* @

EPILOGUE

Robert and Mary were married December 24, 2000. He resigned his job in Huntington, West Virginia and moved to Montpelier. All their dreams are finally coming true. He got another good job, and they bought a house close to Maureen. Mary is staying home taking care of two babies. She and Robert are caring for Tracy's baby girl who was born the same day as baby Lynn. Tracy is still awaiting sentencing. Ralph believes it will be a suspended sentence.

Ralph and Michelle started building a new house in April 2001 and were married the following June. His mother, Fern, and his Uncle Ben are still talking about marriage.

The following Sunday after Ralph's return from Charlotte, he went forward in church and publicly professed Jesus as his personal Savior. He also recited a poem he had written while in Charlotte.

My Goal

Life is a proportion of both good and bad,
With a percentage of happy and sad.
There are seasons of fun and lonely times too,
Measured on a scale from merry to blue.
But sweet peace abounds when I slice the pie,
And serve deeds of love to cheer or hush a cry.
So as days of my life are sliced from the whole,
I pray it's clear to all that Heaven is my goal.

Mason and Mary Ellen still live in West Virginia. They visited Robert and Mary in Vermont two years ago and met Ralph and Michelle. Last year, Robert and Mary went to West Virginia. Robert and Mason went fishing and talked about the good and bad of their lives since the last time they had fished together.

Mary told Robert much more about Alice Johnson. She believed Alice was an angel sent to help her through some difficult times. Alice suddenly appeared at the University as a custodian. So many times she would say the right words of encouragement. They would walk together and shop together, and most importantly, would have long, interesting conversations. Alice could talk about any subject. Mary contributed her survival to Alice, especially after Lynn was born.

Before leaving Boston, Mary went to the University to say goodbye to Alice. She wasn't there, and no one knew anything about her. A search in the files was negative—there was no record of Alice Johnson ever being employed at the University.

Mary shared this with Ralph and Michelle one evening while she and Robert were dining with them. Michelle looked at Ralph and smiled. She then revealed how angels helped her through some difficult times.

ABOUT THE AUTHOR

Harry Beckett is a retired Engineer living in Bar-boursville, WV with his wife, Betty. Harry dreamed of writing a novel during his career of technical writing and his dream came true in 2002 when his first book was published. This book is his fourth with more planned during his retirement.